MW00743551

The Lunenburg Werewolf

And Other Stories of the Supernatural

STEVE VERNON

NIMBUS PUBLISHING

Nimbus Publishing Limited
3731 Mackintosh St, Halifax, NS B3K 5A5
(902) 455-4286 nimbus.ca

Printed and bound in Canada

Author photo: Belinda Ferguson
Cover and interior design: John van der Woude

FSC
www.fsc.org
MIX
Paper from
responsible sources
FSC® C016245

Library and Archives Canada Cataloguing in Publication

Vernon, Steve
   The Lunenburg werewolf : and other stories of the
supernatural / Steve Vernon.
   ISBN 978-1-55109-857-9

1. Ghost stories, Canadian (English)—Nova Scotia. 2. Ghosts—Nova
Scotia. 3. Folklore—Nova Scotia. 4. Haunted places—Nova Scotia.
5. Nova Scotia—History. I. Title.

BF1472.C3V474 2011   398.209716   C2011-903914-1

Nimbus Publishing acknowledges the financial support for its publishing
activities from the Government of Canada through the Canada Book Fund
(CBF) and the Canada Council for the Arts, and from the Province of Nova
Scotia through the Department of Communities, Culture and Heritage.

Contents

Acknowledgements

I'd like to thank Conrad Byers—storyteller, folklorist, and historian from Parrsboro, Nova Scotia—for his invaluable help with "The Tale of the Screeching Bridge."

I'd also like to thank the folks at White Point Beach Resort for inviting me to tell some Halloween stories and for the help they gave me with Ivy's story.

I'd like to thank the folks at Nimbus for the faith they continue to show in my work.

And lastly, as always, I'd like to thank my wife, Belinda, for putting up with me all these years. I could not believe in me if not for thee.

Introduction

~

A STORY, AT THE HEART OF IT, IS AN ANSWER TO A QUESTION. One question I often hear as a storyteller is, "Why do you tell so many ghost stories?" I will be honest. I have never claimed to be a seeker of ghosts. You will not find me hunkered down in a haunted house with an ion counter in one hand, an infrared thermal scanner in the other, and a video camera clenched between my chattering teeth. I am afraid that I am far too lazy for such flagrant adventure. I am nothing more than a storyteller. I weave both history and folklore into the fabric of my yarning in an attempt to entertain whoever has gathered close to the campfire. I am not a historian but I attempt to keep as close to the truth of the matter as humanly possible.

So why ghost stories, then?

I usually answer the question by telling people how I used to listen to my grandfather's stories when I was a boy. I liked his railroad stories, his hunting stories, and his fishing stories, but I loved his ghost stories best. As soon as I heard the rattle of a skeleton, the clatter-clatter of a rusty graveyard chain, or the creaking of a vampire's coffin my ears perked up and opened wide. Ask any kid you know—ghosts are cool.

There is a great tradition of ghost stories here in Nova Scotia. You will find these stories carved in rock, rooted in timber, poured into the water, and wafting through the air that we breathe. The tales are many and varied, ranging from legends of buried pirate treasure, stories of eerie haunted houses and poltergeist pranks, and yarns of mermaids, selkies, and the spirits of the unavenged dead seeking out justice long after the grave has claimed their bones. I tell ghost stories to honour and keep alive this ancient gentle tradition.

One other question that I am asked frequently is, "When are you going to write another collection of Nova Scotian ghost stories?" Well, my first collection, *Haunted Harbours*, has done very well. So it certainly is time for a follow-up to that volume—and you are holding it right here in your clammy little hands.

For this collection I tried to touch on some of the older and more well-known tales, such as the mystery of Oak Island, the tale of the Mary Ellen Spook House in Caledonia Mills, and the haunting of poor Esther Cox of Amherst. Yet I have also spared no effort to unearth some of the lesser-known ghostly yarns of Nova Scotia, such as the tale of the Lunenburg werewolf and the Port Hood story "The Mark of the Fish." Each of the two dozen tales contained in this volume is based on folklore and history that people have been passing around this province for the last two hundred years. The word "story" is just another term for the art of sharing experience. So let my words help you to share the experiences of people from long ago as they attempt to come to grips with the mysteries of the unknown.

From the moment you strike up a conversation with another human being you invariably find yourself talking in stories: "This is how it all got started." "A funny thing happened today." "You won't believe what my mother told me." And so, let me tell you one last story.

I spend a lot of time every year working in Maritime schools through the Writers in the Schools program. I talk to hundreds of kids. I teach them about the shape of the story, how to choose a voice, and how to use that voice well. And then, at nearly every one of my workshops, I like to end with a ghost story. I finish each ghost story with those two wonderful words: "The end."

And then, after I have said those two words the kids will almost always respond with two more: "Tell another."

The Lady in Blue

PEGGY'S COVE

~

APPROXIMATELY FORTY KILOMETRES SOUTHWEST OF DOWNTOWN Halifax lies the little town of Peggy's Cove. The village was founded in the year 1811 when the province of Nova Scotia issued a grant to six families to settle and build up the area. Very little has changed in this tiny fishing village since then—it now has a population of less than one hundred souls, all told.

Over the years, Peggy's Cove has become famous as a kind of living Holy Grail for Nova Scotia tourism. Every year thousands of curious visitors flock from across the globe to walk upon the cove's lonely rocks and search for the Lady in Blue—the ghost of a woman in a blue dress who is said to haunt these shores—and every year the local authorities warn the public of the dangers of clambering over those slippery, wind-blasted boulders. And yet every year—even in the wildest of weather—foolhardy visitors insist upon braving the wave-splashed rocks, risking at best an unexpected dunking and at worst death by drowning.

No one is really sure just how Peggy's Cove originally got its name. Some claim that the name is nothing more than the diminutive of the name Margaret, since Peggy's Cove is situated at the mouth of St. Margaret's Bay. Others will tell you that the tiny village was originally known as Pegg's Cove—as it appears upon maps dating as far back as the late eighteenth century. Storytellers and folklorists will also tell of how, in the early nineteenth century, the town got its name after a sturdy little schooner was shattered upon the glacial granite of Halibut Rock, just a short distance from the current site of the much-photographed Peggy's Cove Lighthouse. Coincidentally, this is also the story of how the Lady in Blue came to haunt the shorelines of this now-infamous tourist attraction.

~

PEGGY'S STORY

IT WAS A STORMY OCTOBER NIGHT. THE WINTRY WIND HOWLED like a mad banshee. The rain sliced down in sheer, horizontal sheets. The local folk called such a storm a Southeaster and on nights like this they laid extra firewood by their hearths, latched their windows, and barred their barn doors securely. Dories were hauled ashore and larger vessels were made fast with the tying on of extra hawser line. However, there was no such protection available for a brave schooner caught in the grip of the open sea.

The schooner's captain leaned heavily against the wheel, pitting his faltering strength against the irresistible power of the current. It was no use.

"We're going to lose her," the first mate told the captain.

"Wrong tense," the captain said. "The fact is we have already lost her."

The first mate shook his head sadly. "Perhaps the men were right, after all," he said. "We should never have allowed a woman on board. It is Jonah luck for certain sure."

"Wrong again," the captain corrected. "The way I count, it looks like we've got two women, not just one."

It was true. The men had threatened mutiny when their captain had first announced that he was allowing a woman to sail with them. To make matters worse, the woman had brought along her young daughter.

In time the men had grown used to these unwanted intrusions. The ill omens promised by their gender were overcome by the woman's kindness and comforting beauty. The men looked forward to watching her walk upon the deck in her favourite dress—a comfortable cotton dyed a particular shade of deep cornflower blue. The sailors even grew used to the sight of her young daughter, the cook would bake her sugar cookies, and the oldest of the men would always find the time each day to play her a tune on his wheezing old concertina.

Yet at a time like this, when the water was roaring and the waves were raging and the wind blew hard enough to blow the pucker from out of a whistle, old feelings would slowly surface.

"Two women on board is twice the bad luck by my mathematics," the first mate pointed out.

"There's no mathematics necessary in a situation like this," the captain said. "Calculate it however you want to and it is nothing more than a matter of time before we all go down and drown."

"So what do we do?" the first mate asked.

"What else can we do?" the captain replied. "Hang on until we can't hang on any longer."

The captain tried his best to bank his foundering vessel and turn her against the relentless current, but it was no use. His grim prophecy of losing the ship proved sadly true as the waves inexorably drove the brave schooner into Halibut Rock. The oak planks of the hull smashed up against the implacable granite with a jolting impact that drove the sailors to their knees. The waves splashed and swallowed the deck. Some of the crew tried to save themselves by clambering atop the schooner's masts.

Meanwhile, one brave sailor saw fit to rescue the ship's female passenger. Whether her presence had brought the vessel to its sorry state or whether it had been simply a mixture of bad timing and bad weather did not matter to this simple sailor. This was a woman in need and he was going to do his level best to see her to safety. "Get up on my shoulders," he told her. "I'll wade to shore."

It was a foolish hope but better than nothing. The woman grabbed her daughter and clung to the brave sailor, who struck out into the current. He kicked away from the sinking schooner and tried his hardest to swim when he realized it was too deep to wade to shore. But the cruel Atlantic current pulled him under, and with his last gasp of strength he pushed the woman a little closer to the shoreline. In turn, she pushed her daughter towards the waiting rocks.

The next morning, when the people of the village came down to survey the aftermath of the shipwreck, they were amazed to find the only survivor—a fifteen-year-old girl who had washed up upon the shoreline.

The trauma of the girl's ordeal had left her suffering with total amnesia. She could not even remember her given name. A local family by the name of Weaver adopted the child and gave her the name Margaret—or Peggy, for short.

~

THE LADY IN BLUE

IT IS SAID THAT YEARS LATER, AS PEGGY WALKED THE SHORELINE, she saw what looked to be a woman in a blue dress—the shade of which was a blend of summer cornflowers, deep sky, and lonely regret. The woman did not seem to walk across the boulders, but rather glided, like a schooner in full sail. Peggy felt a cold breeze shiver across her bones and a salty tear splash at the corners of her vision. As she drew closer, she was amazed to see how strangely familiar the woman looked to her. It was almost as if she were staring into a mirror that had fallen into a quiet tide pool.

"I am sorry," the woman said in a voice as soft as a summer breeze blowing in from the harbour. "I am sorry for leaving you."

Since then the Lady in Blue has been reportedly witnessed by many tourists and residents alike in Peggy's Cove. Some people will tell you that the Lady in Blue is actually the ghost of a woman who married a local man and then grew tired of the life of a wife of a fisherman. She supposedly abandoned her husband and children and sailed away on a Scotland-bound steamer only to sink just a few kilometres from her destination. Since then her spirit is thought to have wandered the rocky shores trying to make amends for her grievous treatment of her family.

Others will agree that the Lady in Blue was a fisherman's wife, but they will add the wrinkle that she wanders the shoreline grieving for her husband, who drowned at sea while trying to support her and her four children on a fisherman's wages. After the incident, she apparently gave her children up for adoption and then in a fit of sorrow starved herself to death, wandering the shoreline and wasting slowly away.

For myself, I believe that the Lady in Blue is the ghost of Peggy's mother—the woman who gave her life so that her child might have a chance of survival. How very much like a mother to never forgive herself for drowning before her daughter was fully grown.

Whatever the story, there are an awful lot of people who have seen this sad blue spirit wandering the lonesome grey rocks of Peggy's Cove. Keep an eye peeled the next time you visit the tiny village named after our heroine—and don't get too close to those grey rocks or those cold, hungry waves.

Murder Island Massacre

YARMOUTH

~

ABOUT TWENTY KILOMETRES SOUTHEAST OF THE TOWN of Yarmouth, in amongst the random scatter of islands that cluster about the larger and better-known Tusket Island—including Green Island, Bald Island, Sheep Island, and Goat Island—lies a bit of rock and timber that is known to the locals as Murder Island. According to Yarmouth historian R. B. Blauveldt, at the time of Yarmouth's first settlement back in 1761, the skeletal remains of an estimated one thousand bodies were discovered bleaching upon the rocky shore of Murder Island.

Some people will tell you that these skeletons were actually the remains of the original diggers of the Oak Island Money Pit, which which we will get to later on in this collection. These people believe that the dreaded Captain Kidd transported all the witnesses of the burial of his treasure to this tiny little island off of Yarmouth, where he murdered them in a fit of cold-blooded savagery.

Several sources also suggest another origin of the name "Murder Island." These sources talk of a great battle that was fought by a pair of warring First Nations tribes upon the island. They report that, according to an eighteenth-century French missionary who spent his life travelling from village to village, the Mi'kmaq and another tribe waged a great battle over a hidden treasure on the island. The resulting massacre was supposedly so brutal that the Mi'kmaq decided the island was bad luck and promptly paddled away from it, leaving it to the bones.

Do not be misled by any books that list this as a possible source for the original name, however, because when I looked into this version of the story, I learned that the sources in question were confusing Murder Island with an island in the St. Lawrence River known as the Île au Massacre (Massacre Island). There, according to local folklore, the Mohawk massacred a band of two hundred Mi'kmaq after trapping them in a small cavern.

So what *really* happened on Murder Island?

~

A DERELICT SHIP

ON THE FINE TUESDAY MORNING OF OCTOBER 7, 1735, THE STURDY two-masted brigantine *Baltimore* set sail from Dublin, Ireland, bound for its home port of Annapolis, Maryland, with approximately five dozen souls on board—including eighteen crewmen and two ship's officers.

The *Baltimore* was sighted once as it rounded Cape Sable Island over a month later. Then, early in December, the ship drifted into Chebogue Harbour, about six kilometres north of Yarmouth. When it arrived, the *Baltimore* was empty of crew and passengers save for a solitary survivor, who called herself Susannah. The deck was stained with blood and hacked in spots as if a great battle had been fought upon it. The ship had quite obviously been ransacked and there were no signs of cargo or valuables.

Susannah identified herself as the wife of the ship's owner, Andrew Buckler. "We were off course," she told the local authorities. "And we dropped anchor at Murder Island to refill our water and to forage for game."

No one thought to ask just why the ship's captain had bothered landing at Murder Island when the larger and more populated Greater Tusket Island was so close at hand. Perhaps they believed that the captain had been confused in his weariness. Perhaps it was just that no one could imagine the possibility that Susannah wasn't exactly telling the whole truth of the matter.

"We were attacked by savage Indians," Susannah went on to explain. "They surprised us at nightfall. They killed the crew and stripped the vessel of everything that could be removed. I managed to survive by locking myself in the captain's cabin. I fought them off with a pair of flintlock pistols that I found hidden in a sea chest in the cabin."

Her rescuers were naturally touched by this story of lone heroism, but there were still a lot of nagging questions that badly needed answering: How had this massacre taken place so close to civilization without being noticed? What were the natives, who had absolutely no history of piracy or massacring shipwreck victims, actually doing out there, so far from their home and hunting ground? What had happened to all the bodies? And why hadn't the attackers, whoever they were, simply broken down the cabin door and overpowered Susannah after her two flintlock pistols were emptied? Unfortunately, Susannah couldn't offer any answers that even came close to satisfying these questions.

"The Indians stripped the vessel of what valuables they could find and departed," she explained. "Afterwards I fainted from fatigue and hunger. I knew nothing until you good people rescued me. I'm afraid that I do not know what became of the bodies of the captain, my husband, and the crew."

She went on to explain that along with seizing the ship's cargo, which she estimated to be valued at about twelve hundred pounds sterling, the mysterious attackers had robbed her of a personal fortune worth sixteen hundred pounds sterling in silver and gold.

"Besides that," she went on. "They stripped the ship of its sails, rigging, furniture, armament, and six fully working swivel guns."

Naturally, the townsfolk did not wish to push a possibly unnecessary interrogation upon the woman. After all, she had barely survived a massacre and had been through a terrifying ordeal. Why punish her further by asking futile questions? She had been through so very much already—hadn't she?

~

THE HOODOO SHIP

AT THE TIME OF SUSANNAH'S ARRIVAL, GOVERNOR LAWRENCE Armstrong was the official in command of Annapolis Royal. In May 1736, Armstrong heard word of the fate of the crew of the *Baltimore* and dispatched Ensign Charles Vane with an armed party to apprehend the mysterious woman who had been found aboard the ship. "We will get to the bottom of this," the governor swore.

Once Vane and the armed party had safely arrested Susannah, they sailed the *Baltimore* back to Annapolis Royal, where they moored her in the harbour. Susannah Buckler appeared before a council and was questioned at length. She repeated her previous story, almost verbatim.

All winter long, the *Baltimore* lay anchored in the harbour. People almost forgot that she was there. As time passed, the ship was stripped of anything worth stealing. She grew a bad reputation, and the local folk began to think of the vessel as some sort of jinx. They gave the *Baltimore* the nickname "The Hoodoo Ship." Some even called it "The Death Ship."

After a time, no one would board, purchase, or sail the ship. Finally, Armstrong ordered the *Baltimore* destroyed. The ill-fated brigantine was towed out to sea, torches were lit and thrown, and the *Baltimore* burned to the water's edge and sank.

Unfortunately, the mystery still remained.

∼

GETTING TO THE BOTTOM OF IT

FINALLY, WORD WAS RECEIVED FROM IRELAND REGARDING THE nature of the passengers on the ship, and the story of what really happened was pieced together. It seemed that the woman who called herself "Susannah Buckler" had actually been a convict, one of sixty convicted criminals who were being transported to Annapolis, Maryland, aboard the *Baltimore*.

During the passage across the Atlantic, "Susannah" had managed to make friends with the ship's owner, Andrew Buckler. Through Buckler she had become acquainted with the captain of the vessel. Before the ship had reached Nova Scotia, "Susannah" had managed to free her fellow convicts, who'd massacred every member of the crew. Afterwards, they'd flung the crewmen's bodies into the water to wash ashore at Murder Island. However, their bloodlust had remained unquenched.

An argument amongst the criminals had somehow escalated into a full-blown battle, and the convicts had killed one another off until only "Susannah" and nine other ex-prisoners remained alive. Then "Susannah" had finished the rest of her comrades off with a pot of salt pork stew—carefully seasoned with rat poison—after which she'd heaved the final nine bodies over the side and into the Atlantic Ocean's cold, merciless grasp.

A perfect crime, or so she'd thought.

SUSANNAH'S FATE

FOLLOWING HER IMPRISONMENT, THE WOMAN KNOWN ONLY AS
"Susannah Buckler" made friends with one of her guards and
eventually escaped from Annapolis Royal. She fled— some believe
with the help of the guard and others believe with the help of a
fisherman—across the border to Boston, where all trace of her
disappeared. Perhaps she died.

Of the booty that was taken from the *Baltimore*, no trace was
ever found. To this day, local fishermen claim to see the spirits
of the massacred men walking the shores of Murder Island by
moonlight and hear strange moans and groans about the shoreline. Some believe that the restless spirits are guarding a hidden
buried treasure, while others believe that these spectres hunger
for a revenge for their unjust slaying.

Sunk by Witchcraft

Pictou

~

IN THE YEAR 1803, A SHIP KNOWN AS THE *FAVOURITE* SANK
mysteriously in the heart of Pictou Harbour. Strangely
enough, as the story goes, the sad catastrophe began with
nothing more than a bad case of indigestion.

The *Favourite* sailed from the port town of Ullapool, Loch
Broom, Scotland, under the command of a Captain Ballantyne.
The ship carried a total of five hundred immigrants, all of them
eager to find themselves a home in Nova Scotia. The *Favourite*
made the journey in a record five weeks and three days, which
was considered by all as a fine omen of good luck to come—which
just shows you how much trust you should put in an omen.

~

A FATAL STOMACH ACHE

IAN WAS A SAILOR—JUST THE SAME AS HIS FATHER AND HIS
father's father before him. "The men in my family have always

worked the sea," Ian would tell anyone who would listen. "We do things one way and one way only—our way—which is fine enough for me." So when Ian signed on as a crewman of the *Favourite*, he was following in the soggy footsteps of his family line and he figured that he could do no wrong.

The *Favourite* arrived in Pictou Harbour with 500 passengers—plus one more. There had been no deaths during the passage, so the birth of a baby had brought the passenger list to 501.

The ship's passengers and crew celebrated their landing in fine Highland style. Ian ate a wee bit too much kidney pie, and no matter how much home-brewed dark ale he tried to wash that kidney pie down with, the fire in his aching belly refused to die.

The townsfolk told him to go and see the old woman who lived in a shack just outside of town. "She knows things," they told Ian. "She will fix you up in no time at all."

The old woman brewed Ian a potent potion of teaberry, burdock, and sweet honey. Then she placed a cold compress over his head and told him to lie still in the cool shade of her cabin until his stomach ache had passed.

"Leave a coin on the kitchen counter when you leave," she told him. "Whatever you feel it is worth is worth enough for me." And then she left to milk the cow.

After a short time, Ian's indigestion passed, and he removed the cold compress and began to think about all of the fun he was missing in town. He dropped the compress on the counter and forgot to give the old woman her payment. Instead he went down to the town, where he danced the night away.

When the old woman returned and found no coin on the counter, her feelings were hurt. She walked down into town and found Ian in a tavern. When she confronted him and demanded her money, he took offence.

"I feel fine now," he told her in no uncertain terms. "In fact, it was your stinking tea that gave me the belly ache in the first place." Which was a bold lie, but Ian had been in that tavern for a little too long and the strong dark ale had run to his head. Being young and foolhardy, he gave the matter no further thought. After all, what did the feelings of one old woman really matter in the long run of things?

～

CURSED BY THE STONE

THAT SAME NIGHT, THE OLD WOMAN WENT OUT BENEATH THE full moon to work a little spell of vengeance magic. She decided that it would serve her needs best if she cursed the ship, rather than the sailor. That way he would live and learn his lesson. Or so she hoped.

She walked along the shore of the harbour, staring at the ship that Ian had sailed in on. "I curse you by the stone," she said aloud. And then she took a stick of charcoal and marked the ship's name upon the stone. She walked three times in a circle, holding the stone high above her head, letting the moonlight wash over it. Then she spat upon the stone three times. Each time she spat, she whispered a word that should never be spoken lightly, a word that had been spoken to her by a demon in the darkest of hours.

When she was finished, the old woman flung the spat-on stone as high and as far as she could. The stone arced above the water, startling a night bird into panicked flight. For just a moment it looked as if the stone might accidentally strike the moon and knock it from its heavenly perch. Then the stone arced downward, hit the cool Atlantic waters of Pictou Harbour, splashed three times, and sank without a trace.

And that night, while Ian and the rest of the ship's crew were singing and making merry in the town tavern, the *Favourite* slid into the waters of Pictou Harbour and sank like a stone.

The next morning, young Ian walked dutifully to the old woman's shanty and laid a silver coin upon her counter. That very same day, every sailor and officer who served on board the *Favourite* did likewise.

Folks in Pictou still talk about the ship that was sunk by witchcraft.

The Phantom Ship of the Northumberland Strait

PICTOU ISLAND

~

THE NORTHUMBERLAND STRAIT IS THAT WIDE WATERWAY that separates the province of Prince Edward Island from New Brunswick and Nova Scotia, stretching a length of 209 kilometres, with a width spanning from 13 to 48 kilometres. Jacques Cartier originally named the passage the Baie de Lunario because he had entered its northern end on July 1, 1534—the day of St. Lunarius. The famous British surveyor Samuel Holland renamed the strait the Red Sea because the water often shone a brilliant blazing red hue at sunrise. However, after a long and lengthy debate, during which it was pointed out that the watery passage in question was neither a bay nor a sea, the government-appointed Canadian Board on Geographical Names settled on naming the passage the Northumberland Strait, after the HMS *Northumberland*, the seventy-gun flagship captained by the famed explorer James Cook. However, what makes this stretch of water curious isn't its name, but the fact that it is home to the best-known and most frequently witnessed ghost ship in all of Nova Scotia—the Phantom Ship of Northumberland Strait.

The Phantom Ship of the Northumberland Strait has been spotted in the Nova Scotia towns of Pictou, Tatamagouche, Wallace, Pugwash, Mulgrave, Inverness, Cheticamp, and Caribou. There are also tales of ship sightings in the Prince Edward Island towns of Alabany, Canoe Cove, Wood Islands, West Point, Murray Harbour, Tignish, Summerside, and Charlottetown. As well, there are stories circulating about sightings in the New Brunswick locales of Richibucto, Buctouche, Shediac, Shippigan, Baie Verte, and Cape Tormentine. The fact is, the Phantom Ship of the Northumberland Strait has been continually spotted and reported along the entire length of the wave-tossed Strait since the late 1700s, when it was first witnessed by wandering Mi'kmaq hunters. And each region and town has its own version of the legend.

Some say that the Phantom Ship is the spectral reappearance of a rich man's pleasure craft. They talk about how, during a drunken brawl on deck, a lamp was upset and exploded into flames. They describe a ghostly cutlass duel that is forever fought on board the Phantom Ship as the flames climb eternally higher.

Others believe that the Phantom Ship is the incarnation of a Scottish immigrant ship bound for Quebec years ago. The ship was blown off course by a howling storm and struck by lightning. Not a soul survived.

Still others, including Helen Creighton in her classic story collection *Bluenose Ghosts*, describe the Phantom Ship as a ball of fire—dark red and glowing like a blacksmith's forge—that slowly takes shape before the onlooker's eyes and transforms into a three-masted schooner. It often appears in the Northumberland Strait when the wind is blowing from the northeast and is frequently witnessed in the harvest months of September and October.

And even others still, mainly those who live along the New Brunswick coastline facing the Northumberland Strait, refer to the Phantom Ship as the "John Craig Light," after a ship named the *John Craig* that was wrecked off of the treacherous, rock-strewn waters of the Shippigan Shoals.

But on Pictou Island in Nova Scotia, fishermen, folklorists, and storytellers have added a completely different element to the mystery: the tale of the Woman in White, who has been seen to walk slowly down to the water to meet the approach of the Phantom Ship of the Northumberland Strait.

～

THE WOMAN IN WHITE

THE WIND HOWLED LIKE A SKY ⁵LLED WITH LONELY, RAVENOUS wolves. The towering black spruce trees leaned and bent with the relentless winds as the waves slapped and splashed the Pictou Island shoreline.

"It is a wild night," Bill Culhane said. "A night when stories beg to be told."

"The wind is doing a fine enough job of stirring up dust," Perry Clifton said, "without your gum-gas and hot air adding to the brew."

"It wasn't blowing on the night when I first saw her," Bill Culhane went on.

That was how Bill always did it. He'd lay a sentence out there that usually didn't seem to have much to do with anything we were talking about. And then he'd just let that sentence dangle, like a well-baited fishing hook, waiting for the first nibble.

Little Jimmy snapped at the bait.

"Saw who?" Little Jimmy asked.

"Now you've done it," Perry said.

"It was calm, you understand," Culhane began. "Calm and eerie. Not a breath stirred in the harbour. The gulls seemed to hover rather than flap. The moon stared down, without a stir of cloud to obscure her glimmer."

"How quiet was it?" Jimmy asked.

"Don't encourage him," Perry moaned, rolling his eyes.

"It was so quiet," Culhane went on, "that you kind of had the feeling that the universe was holding its breath, just waiting to see what happened next."

And that's all he said. Bill Culhane just sat there. Smiling. Waiting.

Little Jimmy was nearly set to burst when Perry finally spoke up. "Well...what happened next?"

"I thought you'd never ask," Culhane replied.

"Get on with it."

So he did. "She'd been waiting for him to sail home," Culhane continued. "Her name was Sheilagh, and she was waiting for young Tommy Hardigan to come back home from the sea."

"And what was he doing out to sea?" Perry asked.

"He was working the water," Culhane explained. "A fisherman, like his father and his father's father before him. Young Sheilagh had sworn that she was going to marry him for certain. 'Tommy Hardigan,' Sheilagh exclaimed. 'If you don't meet me at the church altar before the year is up, I'll swim out and get you, come rain or high water.' Only you've got to be careful what you lay a promise to, because on that windless night Sheilagh looked up and saw the Phantom Ship sailing in on the horizon."

"What did it look like?" Jimmy wanted to know.

"Hush," Perry said.

"All three of the ship's masts were blazing," Culhane said. "And it had skeletons clambering in the rigging, and a set of sails made out of the tanned skins of a hundred dead men—and the wind filling those sails was so cold and lonely that it had to have been blowing from the mouth of hell itself."

"Was Sheilagh scared?" Jimmy asked.

"Scared? Not scared. Sad, more like it. She knew that seeing the Phantom Ship this way meant that Tommy was never coming home again."

"So what did she do?"

"She up and walked down to the water, stepped out into the waves, and waded down into the pounding surf, reaching out in front of her like she was yearning for something that had just barely slipped the stretch of her grasp."

"You're lying," Perry said.

"I'm telling a story," Culhane corrected. And then he went on. "'Get back here,' one man called out. 'You will drown for sure!' But if Sheilagh heard him she gave no sign. She just stared straight ahead as the waves lapped up to her waistline. Three of the bravest spectators splashed out into the water to save her and nearly drowned as the ocean swallowed them whole. But none of these men was half as brave as Sheilagh's daddy. He ran out into the water after her and struck out like he was going to swim all the way to New Brunswick. He was bound and determined to rescue his daughter before she was lost for once and all."

"So what happened?" Jimmy asked. "Did he get her?"

"He did not," Culhane said. "She simply vanished like she was never there."

"Didn't he even get close to her?" Perry asked.

"He did not," Culhane repeated. "Afterwards he swore that he had just managed to touch a single lock of her hair before she slipped away into the current. He claimed that hair had felt like a cold, lonely breeze, chilling him down to his finger bones."

Culhane shivered theatrically and Little Jimmy shivered right along with him.

"The hand had seized up, right then and there," Culhane went on. "He couldn't bend a joint in his finger, not even with a set of cold iron pliers. He spent the rest of his days sitting and shivering by his kitchen fire, trying to keep warm. Even in the hottest of summers, you would find the man sitting there with the flames roaring up like Jimmy-Be-Jeepers."

Now it was Perry's turn to shiver.

"For the rest of his natural life, the ache in the fingers and bones of his right hand never left the man a moment of peace," Culhane continued. "And every time the joints would creak and twinge and ache, he would shiver as he remembered the sight of his daughter walking out into that cold, lonely sea."

"Liar," Perry spat.

"Liar back at you," Culhane retorted. "My granddaddy told me this story and something else besides. He swore that he was out there at the harbour side watching at the last of it. He saw her clamber up the boarding net that those skeleton-ghosts hung for her over the side of the Phantom Ship. He watched her clamber up like a sailor with monkey blood running through her veins. The cold blaze dried her dripping form as the blue fire rose and crackled and sung through the long tresses of her hair."

"What did she do then?" Little Jimmy wanted to know.

"She took her place at the bow of the ship, and stiffened into a figurehead that both leaned away and sang towards the lost and lonely crew of the Phantom Ship of the Northumberland Strait."

For a half a moment everyone in the room sat and held their breath.

Finally, being the youngest and least patient of the lot, Little Jimmy spoke.

"Is that a true story?" he asked Culhane.

Culhane fixed Little Jimmy with a look that could freeze a fully grown furnace.

"It's a story, truly told."

～

A RECENT SIGHTING

IN MID-JANUARY 2008, SEVENTEEN-YEAR-OLD MATHIEU GIGUERE stepped out from a local Tatamagouche gym to catch his breath.

He stared out across the ice-locked mid-winter stretches of Tatamagouche Bay and was amazed to realize that he was looking at an unbelievably eerie sight—a vessel where no ship could possibly be, sailing calmly through a field of ice.

"It was bright white and gold, and it looked like a schooner with three masts," Mathieu said. "Just like the *Bluenose*."

The sight was, in a word, impossible. The ship that Mathieu described was a sailing vessel of a sort that hadn't been witnessed in Tatamagouche Bay for well over a hundred years. And there was no way that it could have sailed through that ice-bound harbour.

Mathieu stared at the glowing vessel for several minutes before returning inside to the gym. After he had completed his workout, he came back outside and was surprised to see that the vessel had disappeared completely, in spite of the ice-locked condition of the harbour.

A short time later, the details of Mathieu's sighting were noted and corroborated by local artist Barb Gregory at her Bay Head establishment, the Phantom Ship Art Gallery. It seems that young Mathieu took one look at the artist's rendition of the Phantom Ship—a painting that she had developed through careful research of dozens of previously recorded sightings of the mysterious spectral vessel—and recognized it immediately. And so Mathieu's sighting joined a long line of ghostly sightings stretching back through the centuries.

~

A MISINTERPRETATION OF SQUID

SO IS THERE ANY SINGLE SCIENTIFIC REASON BEHIND THE sightings of this eerie flaming leviathan? Some researchers believe that the encounters are nothing more than a sort of mirage conjured by the glint of the setting sun over the water, which is perhaps enhanced by the silhouette of tall spruce trees as seen through the common and deceptive filter of sea fog. Others believe that the apparitions of the ship are caused by the release of methane gas, trapped under the dozens of coal beds beneath Nova Scotia waters.

These underwater methane deposits are also blamed for the booming sounds of the "sea guns," which some people believe to be the cannons of a ghostly pirate vessel—often the Phantom Ship itself. The presence of sea guns has been reported as many times as the Phantom Ship has been sighted, if not more. The guns are usually heard rumbling across the water in a series of three to six cannonades—*boom, boom, boom*. The sound of the guns is often accompanied by an eerie splash of light, which gives credence to the theory that both the sea guns and the flaming Phantom Ship are nothing more than the by-products of exploding methane gas.

There is yet another argument on the nature of the Phantom Ship, which states that the many and varied sightings of the eerie glowing ship are an optical illusion caused by squid ink. Certain scientists claim that when panicked by attack, schools of squid will produce an abundance of blackish-brown phosphorescent ink. It is believed that the combination of wind, water current, and static electricity acting upon the glowing ink creates the illusion of a giant phantom vessel.

Squid, sunshine, and the flatulence of saltwater coal are certainly intriguing theories. However, the truth of it is that nobody knows for sure what really causes the Phantom Ship to appear.

The Mare of McNabs Island

HALIFAX

~

WEDGED LIKE A FISH BONE IN THE THROAT OF HALIFAX Harbour lies McNabs Island, the location of many strange incidents and coincidences throughout history, and the setting of many local storytellers' ghost stories.

One of the island's most prominent features is the long, tenuous point that juts out from it into the belly of the harbour like the blade of an open jackknife. Back in the eighteenth century, the point was known as Deadman's Beach on account of the many skeletons found scattered and strewn upon its rocky shore when the British first settled in 1749. These skeletons were rumoured to be the remains of the French invasion fleet of 1745, captained by the unlucky Duc D'Anville, whose story is more properly told in my book *Halifax Haunts*. It is estimated that Duc D'Anville lost over a thousand men to fever, shipwreck, and storms. Many of the dead were simply and unceremoniously cast into the harbour with a cannon ball knotted to their feet.

In March 1753, Deadman's Beach and the salt marsh that surrounded it were deeded to one Joshua Mauger, a seafaring merchant with a bad reputation for smuggling rum and contraband. The point was known as Mauger's Beach until the British raised a gallows at the end of the beach. These gallows gave birth to the nickname that hangs on the point to this very day: Hangman's Beach.

Further down McNabs Island, towards the mouth of Halifax Harbour, broods the Thrumcap Shoal—a nasty hook of submerged rock that tore the belly out of the Royal Navy frigate HMS *Tribune* on November 16, 1797, and took her and over two hundred sailors to the bottom of the harbour.

It was from this point that poor Peter McNab IV stared out one hot August morning in 1853 and watched as a sea serpent, nearly six metres long with an evil nub of a head, writhed and twisted through the white-capped waves. Whether or not the sea monster was to blame, McNab died screaming in Mount Hope Asylum twenty years later.

There are many more stories attached to McNabs Island—stories of murder and mayhem and things that go bump in the night—but none is more mysterious than the tale of Dermot McGregor and his piebald mare.

~

BROKEN DREAMS

THE SUMMER THUNDER DRUMMED AND RUMBLED OVER THE length of McNabs Island. A crackle of heat lightning split the July night sky, and Dermot McGregor's head felt like it was going to burst apart from the headache that was coming on. Dermot was a short man with a shorter temper and a shock of red hair that made it look as if his head had caught alight.

The children were crying again. It seemed like they were always crying about something. Six-year-old Elias had been tug-of-warring with three-year-old Mara over their favourite toy stick. Only the stick had snapped, Elias had fallen, and Mara had jammed a willow splinter deep into her thumb.

"Let me take a needle to that splinter," Dermot's wife, Annie, said to Mara. "If I leave it you'll weep for seven long years." Which only made Mara cry all the louder.

Dermot looked longingly out the kitchen window. "Sometimes I think I'd like to just get off of this lousy little island," he said to Annie. "And away from everything that is bound to drag me down."

Annie did her very best to humour his morose complaining while trying to simultaneously juggle a pair of constantly crying children, a very hungry and smelly dog, and a needy and slightly gone-to-seed husband. "Are you planning to go to Halifax, then?" she asked with half a grin. She had heard him sing this tired old tune many a time. Dermot was a dreamer who had never quite learned to be happy with the fate life had dealt him. He always felt that he was missing out on some better dream, just a little over the horizon. "Be sure to take me with you when you go. I need to buy some new blue ribbon."

"I'm not just talking about Halifax," Dermot grumbled. "There is a whole big old world out there waiting for me, just out beyond those waves."

"And what are you going to use for money?" Annie asked. "You're a little short on looks and long on debt as far as I can see."

"I have a plan," Dermot said mysteriously.

"I was afraid you'd say that."

Dermot always had some sort of a plan—which didn't necessarily mean that he knew just what he was doing while he was doing it.

"Tommy Crowse says he knows where some treasure is buried at."

Annie snorted her disdain.

"If Tommy Crowse told me that fire will burn you, I'd still most likely want a second opinion."

"Tommy Crowse is a very smart man."

"Tommy Crowse doesn't know if he was born, hatched, or planted," Annie said. "If shoes were clues, that man would walk about barefoot."

"He's seen it himself," Dermot insisted. "Five stones under a cherry tree, halfway up the side of Strawberry Hill. He swears that those stones were put there by pirates."

"Any pirate with half an ounce of brain would spend what treasure he had in the tavern rather than bury it where any idiot could dig it up."

"That's not what a pirate does," Dermot argued.

"And what would you know about pirates?"

At this point in the argument, Dermot was not about to be swayed by anything remotely resembling common sense. He had hit upon a plan and was bound to see it through.

"It's a treasure map," Dermot said. "Tommy Crowse traded Billy Bulger a nearly full bottle for it."

"Well, why in blue bloody blazes would Billy Bulger trade a treasure map for a nearly empty bottle of gin?"

"It was rum!" Dermot roared. "And I told you the bottle was nearly full. Besides, what good would treasure do old Billy—what with him being half-blind and near-illiterate to boot?"

"Would you listen to yourself talk?" Annie asked.

"I'm not listening," Dermot snapped. "Consider me deaf as a knothole post to whatever you have to say."

"A fine stew it is that you're brewing," Annie said, with a laugh. "The blind leading the deaf and the dumb."

Dermot shook his head in confusion. "How can you call Tommy Crowse dumb?" he asked. "Tommy talks just as fine as paint."

"Tommy Crowse can talk the ears off a dead moose," Annie said. "And I'm looking straight at the only man dumber."

That did it. Dermot slammed the door. Annie opened the door and slammed it again after him.

Dermot jumped on his old piebald mare. He missed and fell in the mud. He climbed back up while Annie watched from the window, trying hard not to laugh. By now even young Elias and his sister Mara had come to the window and were trying just as hard, only not nearly as successfully—which didn't help Dermot's temper one bit.

Dermot dug his heels into the mare's mottled rump, clicked his tongue against the edge of his teeth, and galloped off down the old Cliff Trail, aiming himself straight at Hangman's Beach.

"Where's Daddy going?" Elias asked, balancing on his toes by the windowsill in order to have a better look.

"Is he going for a ride?" Mara asked around a mouthful of splinter-stuck thumb.

"Your father has hitched up his sadly wounded dignity and taken it for a long hard gallop," Annie said. "And it's time you both were in bed."

A half hour later, once the children were both asleep, Annie went back to the window, peered out into the night, and shook her head. Her man most likely wouldn't be back until morning, when he would come stealing in—most likely with a fistful of freshly picked dandelions, daisies, and buttercups—meekly asking after his breakfast.

Dermot wasn't a bad man, only bad-tempered and inclined to bouts of unpredictable stupidity. Annie knew very well that he was just trying in his own simple-minded way to find a better life for their children. *Foolish man*, she thought to herself. *Doesn't he know that life is as good as it gets so long as you're left alive to live it?*

Annie lit a tall white candle and placed it gently in the window in case Dermot found his way home that night. Then she sat down in her old willow rocker, tilting it back and letting it slide forward, rocking herself down to an untroubled sleep.

The candle flame flickered and danced. The wind blew cool under the window. The old cotton curtains shifted with the hot July breeze. Annie slept on dreamlessly.

PIRATE'S GOLD AND PENNIES APLENTY

DERMOT GALLOPED UP TO TOMMY CROWSE, WHO WAS STANDING at the foot of Strawberry Hill with a lantern in one hand and a pick in the other. Dermot nearly threw himself from the mare and tried his best to make it look as if that was how he had originally intended to dismount.

"Have a care with all that tearing about," Tommy warned him. "You gallop like that and you're apt to make a ghost out of yourself."

Tommy crossed himself from habit at the word "ghost."

"Have you got the map?" Dermot snapped.

"No," Tommy said. "I left it at home for safe keeping with my old tomcat. *Of course I brought the map!*"

Tommy held up the map, nearly shattering the lantern with the blade of the pick.

"Careful, yourself," Dermot scolded. "You catch the map alight and we'll all go penniless."

"No fear of that, man," Tommy said, hastily dropping the pick in the dirt. "There will be pirate's gold and pennies a plenty when this night is done."

Pennies. That was really what this whole thing was about. It hurt Dermot deeply to watch Annie eke out a bare minimum existence, counting every penny. He didn't like that he couldn't afford to dress her in finery. He didn't like that they had to depend upon the berry harvest and the rabbits he could snare to feed the kids. He didn't like that his children couldn't afford to play with anything better than a stick. All that Dermot wanted was a better life for his family. Was that so much to ask?

"The map says one hundred paces north of the oak tree," Tommy read aloud. The oak tree was easy. It was the biggest tree in Hangman's Marsh.

"All right, navigator," Dermot said. "So which way is north?"

Tommy looked about to his left and right.

"I think that's the North Star," Tommy said, pointing straight up.

"Well, isn't it a shame that I forgot to bring my sky-walking boots?"

"Is there any moss on the side of the oak?" Tommy asked. "Moss always grows on the north side."

"We're in the middle of a marsh," Dermot pointed out. "And as far as I can see there is moss all around here."

Tommy thought about that.

"Uphill," he finally decided.

"Come again?"

"North is up on the map, isn't it?" Tommy said. "And the North Star is up in the sky. So it stands to reason that if we pace uphill, we're bound to hit north."

It was a little too late for thinking so hard about such matters. Dermot stuck his finger straight ahead, pointing uphill. "Lead on, navigator," he said.

The two men began trudging uphill, counting each pace as they went. "One, two, three, four, five..."

"Whatever you do, don't look up," Tommy warned. "There's a full moon tonight and it's fearful bad luck if you stare at the moon through the fork of a tree."

"Tommy, we're in the middle of a forest," Dermot pointed out. "How else are we going to look at the moon, if we aren't staring up through branches?"

"Well all the same, don't go looking," Tommy said. "That's when a ghost will sneak up on you—while you're staring at the moon."

Dermot's old mare blew her breath through her lips as he pulled her up the hill. She reeked of hay and horse sweat. Secretly, Dermot was glad he had her along with him. In a way she kind of comforted him. "There's no such thing as ghosts," Dermot said.

"Eleven, twelve, thirteen, fourteen, fifteen..."

"That shows you just what you know," Tommy said. "Why, it wouldn't surprise me one bit if one reached out and grabbed the both of us right now."

"Twenty, twenty-one, twenty-two, twenty-three, twenty-four, twenty-five…"

"So how are you going to spend all the gold we find?" Tommy asked.

"Once we find it," Dermot corrected.

"I'd like to go back home to the old country," Tommy went on as if Dermot hadn't said a word. "I'd like to open up a tavern and keep the door locked all day long and just drink my worries away."

Dermot laughed. That sounded a lot like Tommy's kind of thinking.

"Well, what would you do with your money?" Tommy asked.

"I'd like to give my family a better life. I'd like to see them in a better place with all that a family ever needs. I'd like to buy Annie dresses and little Elias and Mara some proper toys."

"What's wrong with a toy stick?" Tommy asked. "That's all you and I ever had to play with."

Dermot counted pennies for paces as they hiked up the hill, hungry for a pirate's buried treasure—which was why he tripped over his feet and fell face-first halfway up the hillside. He reached forward as he fell and inadvertently caught hold of Tommy's left heel.

"He's got me!" Tommy howled aloud, thinking he was being attacked by ghosts. "He's got me by the heel!"

Before Dermot could say a word, Tommy up and ran, kicking off his boots and screaming out into the darkness, looking for all the world as if he were figuring on running barefoot back to the old country.

Dermot tried to call him back, but it was too late. He shook his head and grinned. "I hope he stops running before he hits the water," he said to himself, shaking his head sadly. "And he took the map with him. Well this was a wasted night, for sure."

The old mare blew her breath out through her lips as if she secretly agreed with Dermot.

"Come on then, horse," Dermot said. "Let's get ourselves home. Annie will be waiting to laugh at me in the morning."

Dermot turned the horse around. He glanced up through the branches of the tree ahead and saw the full moon looking down at him—the full moon and something else a whole lot brighter. The sky was lit up as if the stars themselves had caught on fire.

Dermot knew what it was right off. "Annie," he whispered.

Then he leaped up on the old mare's back and kicked his heels hard.

〜

A LEGACY OF ASHES

THE OLD MARE GALLOPED A SECOND TIME INTO THE DARKNESS. The light in the distance tore up at the sky. Dermot leaned in and urged a little more speed from the old nag. At this rate, if the mare threw him, he would break his neck for certain. As it was, he might run the horse into a tree and break both their necks. He didn't care. "Faster," he whispered.

The old mare galloped like she had never galloped before.

But Dermot was too late.

When he got back to his home, it had burnt to the ground. The candle that Annie had left burning in the window had caught on the cotton curtains, and the fire had raced through the old cottage like a galloping stallion. There was nothing left but a legacy of cinder and ashes.

Dermot knelt in the ashes of his home. He wept a long time, until something caught his eye. He picked it up.

It was little Elias and Mara's toy stick, somehow spared from the flames. Dermot squeezed the stick until white half-moons of frustrated tension shone on the backs of his fingernails.

Then he climbed grimly onto the back of his tired, piebald mare and brought the stick down hard and sharp against the old horse's haunches. "Giddy up," Dermot cried.

He rode down along the old Cliff Trail. He rode past the foolish buried treasure dreams of Strawberry Hill. He rode headlong down the length of Hangman's Beach. He hit the pounding waves and kept on riding, straight into the deep black waters.

To this day people will talk about how you will see the flicker of a candle and a roaring flame in the heart of the dark McNabs Island wood. They will tell you that it is a ghostly memory of an orphanage that burned down a long time ago. They will tell you how there is a treasure buried on the island and no one has ever found it. They will tell you of how you will hear ghostly hoof beats galloping down the old Cliff Trail. They will tell you all of these tales as if they were three completely separate stories. Only a few know the truth behind the matter—that all of these tales are linked together like a single unyielding chain anchored in dreams, ambition, and a fool's bitter regret.

The Kentville Phantom Artist

KENTVILLE

~

I F YOU TRAVEL JUST ONE HUNDRED KILOMETRES FROM
Halifax, you will come to the town of Kentville. In the early
nineteenth century, the town's centralized location, on the
hub of several roadways and coach routes and eventually a train
line, made it a popular spot for wayfaring travellers. Kentville
soon developed a reputation for rowdy drinking and horse racing, earning it the nickname "the Devil's half acre." The locals
can tell you many intriguing tales of depravity and debauchery
that took place in this era, but the most curious of them all is the
story of a young painter's brush with fate.

~

A SHORTAGE OF ROOMS

THE LEAVES WERE FALLING, ONE BY ONE, LIKE TATTERED SCRAPS
of some unfinished painting. It was autumn in Kentville. A

travelling art supply salesman by the name of Walter Irving arrived in town on the train, encumbered with an overstuffed suitcase and three bulging sample trunks. He had come from Halifax, where he had been visiting his poor mad sister in the mental asylum. The girl had been committed the previous summer. Her senses had left her one night while she was sleeping. They found her in the morning giggling ceaselessly.

"I saw a ghost," she'd sworn. "A painted ghost."

Walter shook his head at the thought of it.

He was tired and hungry and ready for rest—only it seemed as if rest would be hard to come by.

"There's an awfully big horse race going on in Kentville this weekend," the conductor told him. "You're going to have some trouble finding a place to stay."

It turned out the conductor's prediction was dead right.

"I'm afraid that I've only got one room left," the hotel owner told Walter. "I've let it out to a friend of mine from Shelburne, but I am sure he wouldn't mind sharing. How would that suit you?"

"That would suit me right down to my bones," Walter answered.

"Have you had supper yet?" the owner asked him.

Walter sat down at a table with about forty men who were mostly interested in talking about the horse race. He finished his meal of stew and dumplings and chased it with a strong cigar and a pint or two of ale.

When Walter finished his dinner, he said his good nights and went directly to his room. He opened the door and was surprised to see a slender young man sitting upon the golden chaise lounge with a large leather portfolio balanced upon his lap. The youth was pale, inordinately so, and his skin seemed nearly transparent.

Of course, Walter thought to himself. *This must be the guest from Shelburne that the owner spoke about.*

"My name is Walter Irving," Walter introduced himself, entering the room and bolting the door behind him. "I represent a firm that deals in art supplies."

"A peddler, eh?" the young man replied with a charming wry grin as he open his portfolio. "And of art supplies? What a coincidence. I sketch a bit myself. My name is George Cushman."

"An artist, are you?" Walter asked.

"Only an amateur," George replied. "Would you like to see some samples of my latest work?"

Walter sat for over an hour, studying the young man's artwork. The majority of the sketches were rough, yet they showed a deep and genuine talent. There was an authenticity to George's pencil work, a certain quality that seemed to linger and haunt the salesman.

"Look as much as you like," George said. "You may even keep them if you like. Where I am bound for, I will have no need of sketches. As for me, I believe it is finally time to seek my rest." The young man stretched out upon the chaise lounge, closed his eyes, and fell into a sleep so deep that Walter could detect barely a trace of respiration.

Mesmerized, Walter continued to flip through the artwork. There were countless views of the Cornwallis River and the surrounding countryside—landscapes and portraits and roughed-out sketches. Walter was most struck by a portrait of a beautiful young woman with eyes that seemed to gleam like moonlit ice. She was smiling in such a way that seemed to promise laughter.

I've seen this face before, Walter thought.

He placed the portrait beside his luggage. In the morning he would ask the young man if he could keep it. After all, hadn't George said that he could take whatever pieces interested him?

∼

A GHOSTLY VISITATION

WALTER IRVING BLEW OUT THE FLAME OF HIS BEDSIDE CANDLE and lay there in the darkness. The bird's-eye maple panelling seemed to stare at him from the shadowed darkness, and from atop his luggage the face of the mysterious woman seemed to glisten and shine.

The next morning Walter woke up to find that young George had disappeared in the night. At first he was certain that the young man had robbed him, but when he checked, his belongings seemed intact. Even the portrait of the woman had not been touched.

Yet strangely, the door was still bolted from the inside.

Had George climbed out the window? Walter checked the window, but it was securely fastened.

Walter sat down upon his bed and puffed upon a morning cigar, trying to make some kind of sense out of the mystery. Then he rose and dressed and went downstairs to inquire as to the whereabouts of his roommate.

"Your friend from Shelburne seems to have vanished," he told the hotel owner.

"In fact, he never arrived," the owner replied. "His stage was delayed. I had told him to take the train, but he is stubborn like that. I found out so late in the evening that I did not think to trouble you and let you know, assuming you had already gone to sleep."

"But what about the young artist who stayed with me?" Walter asked. "What about George Cushman?" He told the owner what had happened that night, then retrieved the portrait of the woman from his pocket as proof. When he showed the owner the portrait, the man turned ashen.

"I am afraid that you were sleeping next to a ghost last night," the owner said. "The truth is, George Cushman hung himself in that very room."

"Why didn't you warn me?" Walter asked.

"I'm trying to run a hotel," the owner explained. "If I were to warn every one of my customers about every bad doing that has gone on in these rooms, I might as well hang a 'Hotel for Sale' sign on the front door."

The man did have a point.

"Why did he hang himself?" Walter finally asked.

"He couldn't find a pistol, I expect."

"You owe me a better answer than that."

The owner nodded. "I guess I do," he admitted. "Do you see that woman in the picture? She's pretty enough, I suppose, but the sad truth is that she was the cause of it all."

"Who was she?" Walter asked.

"Her name was Alice."

"Is she still alive?"

"The last I heard she was living in an insane asylum up in Halifax. I hear she's taken out a long-term lease."

That's when it hit him. Walter knew just where he had seen that woman before. In the cell beside his sister at the Halifax asylum.

"Incurable?" Walter asked.

"Irrevocable," the owner replied.

"Tell me the story."

"George Cushman was the son of a wealthy New York businessman," the owner began. "He was an artist, by all accounts. That's always a bad sign. A man gets to messing his mind up with imagination and such and there is no telling what end it will lead him to. He used to paddle a canoe up and down the Cornwallis River. I'd see him out there with an easel set up, painting his landscapes."

The owner shook his head ruefully. "The darned fool should have known better. One day the canoe caught a snag and turned keel-over-kettle. It nearly drowned him. Alice pulled him out. She was the daughter of a fisherman, and Lord knew the trouble that she caught that day."

"What happened?" Walter asked. "Did he fall in love?"

"He jumped in, was more like it. You know these artistic types. Intense is the word. He fell in love with Alice right then and there. He made his mind up that the two of them were going to live together happily ever after. He decided they would raise up a whole house-load of budding young art students. Too bad he didn't think to let the girl in on his plans."

The owner looked down at the painting. "He caught her at a garrison ball, dancing with a young officer. He quarrelled with her. He made such a scene that three of the troopers threw him out into the street. He came back to this hotel and he hid up in his room for three whole days. On the third day he hung himself. It was Alice who found him, the way I heard it. I guess she'd come to apologize for offending his brittle imagination."

"It must have been bad for her," Walter said.

"Bad?" the owner said. "It was outright ugly. She had no idea what was going on in his head. We found her sitting there in the scraps of his artwork, kneeling before his noosed-up corpse. Her hands were clasped white-knuckle tight and she was staring at the wall, not seeing a blessed thing. She hasn't spoken a word since then, as far as I know. I expect she's most likely sitting up there in her room in the asylum, still staring at the walls."

Walter looked down at the portrait. The eyes seemed to follow him. "I think we ought to burn it," he said.

So they laid a fire in the main fireplace and when the flames were crackling high enough Walter placed the portrait upon the fire. The flames licked and crackled upon the canvas. One would have thought that the oil-laden fabric would have easily kindled, but oddly, the painting proved resistant to fire. When the firewood died down into a bed of cinders and ash, the owner removed the cursed portrait.

"The flames haven't touched it," he said.

There was not even a trace of smoke damage.

"What will you do with the picture?" Walter asked.

"I will store it in the attic," the owner replied. "She was a guest once, and I will make her welcome for as long as she needs to stay."

And the painting is there still.

Beast of the Black Ground
GRANDE ANSE

D EEP IN THE HEART OF CAPE BRETON'S RICHMOND County, midway down Highway 4, lies the quiet little town of Grande Anse. Legend has it that if you travel along the Grandique Ferry Road approximately one kilometre from Grand Anse, you will come to a clearing. There, framed by a border of tall black spruce standing so stock still that they seem to be holding their needled breath and waiting for something to crawl out of that darkness, is what the local folk will fearfully tell you is the Black Ground.

The Black Ground is a sprawling field bisected by the nasty slashing scar of a long dirt road. There is a lake at one end of the field that some people believe to be bottomless. A series of wildfires have blazed through the field over the centuries and as a result the soil has blackened with ash. The blueberries and cranberries that grow in the field are known to be fat and juicy, but very few locals will dare to pick them.

Many believe that the Black Ground is haunted by a Bochdan—an ancient beast that came across the ocean from its Scottish homeland, stowed away on a ship of early settlers. A Bochdan is a kind of hobgoblin that feeds on fear and carrion. The Bochdan lives for mischief and mayhem of the darkest kind. It cloaks itself in shadow and favours sour ground. It hides in brooks and peers up at unwary wanderers just before reaching up suddenly and dragging them down to drown.

The older folk who live in the surrounding regions of the Black Ground swear they've seen inhuman figures dancing there in the darkness. They claim to have heard beastly sounds of baying out there beneath the moonlight, sounds that chilled their blood and caused their hearts to skip a beat or two.

They say that there was once a settlement on the Black Ground. People lived there and grew content in the belief that they could turn its cursed soil to good. But all that changed when two young Cape Breton boys witnessed a terrifying midnight parade.

~

PLANS AND BLUEBERRIES

ONE LONG, HOT, AND DUSTY AUGUST AFTERNOON, HAROLD and Franklin Dunbar set out to pick blueberries on the Black Ground. But the blueberry picking soon gave way to a game of hide-and-seek, which just as naturally gave way to a sudden bout of tree-climbing, which of course led the boys to an hour-long ponder over the best location to build themselves a tree fort. Which was right about the time that darkness fell onto them like a great panther leaping down onto the back of an unwary traveller.

Out here on the Black Ground, the charred dirt seemed to gulp down any trace of light. Even the moon and the stars seemed to blur and haze and shrink against the bleak black of that stretch of cursed Cape Breton wilderness.

"Can you see much?" Harold asked.

"Not much more than you can, I expect," Franklin answered.

Which was right about the moment when something out there in the darkness screeched. It might have been a screech owl. It might have been a wild cat. It might even have been nothing but a long fir bough fiddling against a patch of tuneful tree bark. Or it might have been a ghost.

"We ought to light a fire," Franklin said.

"Are you sure?" Harold asked. "The brush out here is awfully dry for lighting fires."

Harold spoke the truth. It had been two weeks since the last rainstorm had soaked the surrounding woodland, and it was quite likely that a poorly laid camp blaze would risk a forest fire.

"I don't care," Franklin said. "I want a fire."

"You're scared, aren't you?"

Which was right about when that whatever-it-was in the darkness screeched out a second time, even louder than the first.

Goosebumps waddled across a pair of scared young necks. Hair started to rise. Hearts beat at a double-gallop. And fear crept on in.

"Of course I'm not scared," Franklin replied with a hastily swallowed gulp. "I am absolutely wet-my-pants-and-scream-like-a-little-girl terrified. 'Scared' just isn't nearly a big enough word for the way that I feel right now."

"It's good to know I'm not the only one who is scream-like-a-little-girl terrified," Harold replied as he scraped the fir needles away from a patch of dirt and started scooping out a firepit. "You get the wood and I'll lay the fire."

Franklin looked fearfully out into the darkness, waiting for one more screech. "How about you get the wood and I lay the fire?" he asked.

"I've got the matches," Harold said. "So you need to go and get the wood."

Which made a whole lot of sense, as much as Franklin hated to admit it. So off Franklin went to gather up as much dead wood as he could bundle into his arms. Harold stayed behind to lay the beginnings of a small campfire.

Harold looked up once as Franklin walked away. He was worried for his friend, but he would not let himself stare too long, because everyone knew that to stare too long at someone leaving was bad luck and a surefire guarantee that you would never see that someone alive again. Which didn't comfort Harold in the least.

Harold busied himself with clearing away anything that might accidentally burn to prevent the risk of wildfire. He laid rocks about the fire pit and clawed up and scooped out what dry grass, twigs, and birch and pine bark that he could find close at hand.

Franklin soon came back with an armload of sticks. The boys set up their wood, and then Harold retrieved his matches and lit the kindling. With a small patch of light to cut into the oppressing darkness, the boys let out a sigh of relief.

Which was about when a cold wind whooshed down suddenly across the Black Ground. The campfire blew out like a birthday candle. Harold and Franklin huddled in the unexpected darkness.

Franklin reached out impulsively and touched the cinders of the fire. "They're as cold as December icicles," he whispered. "They ought to be warm just a little bit, oughtn't they?"

Which was right about when they heard the sound coming from out of the darkness—a scuttling, like the sound of a thousand crabs moving across a beach of broken clamshells. The wind blew a little harder. Harold and Franklin suddenly smelled a funk, a stench so foul that it stank worse than a thousand mildewed rubber boots turned wrong-side out.

Both the boys froze.

"Look," Harold whispered. He pointed into the darkness.

Franklin stared in horrified awe as three ancient hags teetered out of the cloying darkness. "Night hags," he breathed in terror.

Now for those of you who don't know, a night-hag is what you find left over after a witch is hanged. The witches' shadows, if they are not properly sprinkled in holy water and holly berries, will rise up and haunt the night, eating whatever they can find in hopes of filling their emptiness.

The three night hags, their backs bent like question marks, scuttled and crawled across the Black Ground, pausing to claw up handfuls of herbs and grass, which they crammed into their constantly chewing mouths. Franklin and Harold could hear the noise of their ceaseless munching, like the sound of horses eating hay.

"I smell boy," the first old hag said suddenly.

"I smell two boys," the second hag said as she casually reached up and plucked a small owl from the bough of an overhanging tree and crammed it—feathers and all—into the wood-chipper maw of her mouth.

"I smell them too," the third hag croaked. "And they're hiding just behind that alder bush."

Which was right exactly where Franklin and Harold were hiding.

"Do you think we can outrun those three night hags?" Franklin whispered.

"I'm not worried about outrunning them," Harold whispered back. "I just figure all I have to do is outrun you."

The two boys took off like a pair of scalded cats. The trio of night hags followed the boys, not really running but rather passing over the Black Ground like shadows, cutting Harold and Franklin off whichever direction they turned.

"Run the other way!" Harold screamed.

"Which other way?" Franklin screamed back.

In the panic and dizzying confusion of their breakneck run, Harold and Franklin had headed straight to the shore of the dark lake. They looked down into the water and were terrified to see something rising up out of the darkness towards them—something with a goat's head and a horse's body and a set of teeth that looked like a mouthful of cutlasses and rusty cleavers.

"The Bochdan!" the boys screamed out simultaneously. They turned to run, only to find themselves facing the three night hags, who were hovering straight toward them.

"We're going to die!"

And then, as quick as you could say, "snip-snap-gulp," the Bochdan swallowed the three night hags whole.

The boys stood there in the darkness, their knees knocking together in a state of pure and total fear. Too scared to run. Too scared to even think of running.

The Bochdan leaned down and sniffed at Franklin. "Too skinny-thin," it said in a voice of tombstone and thunder.

And then it leaned towards Harold. "Go home and grow some more," the Bochdan told them.

Which is right around the time those boys started running.

The Quit-Devil

GLACE BAY

~

IN THE EARLY EIGHTEENTH CENTURY, THE FRENCH COLO-
nized a small area around a harbour on the northeastern
side of Cape Breton. The plan was to use the little settlement as a source of ready coal for their mighty fortress in
Louisburg. They named the spot the "Baie de Glace"—the "Bay of
Ice"—because they found that the harbour froze over completely
every winter.

By the mid 1940s, Glace Bay, as it became known, had grown
into the most heavily populated town in the entire country of
Canada. It was a town of coal miners—born storytellers—who told
tales of dark deeds that took place in the shadows of the tunnels. Many have these stories have since been lost, but one tale the
coal miners of Glace Bay will never forget is the story about a boy
named Randy and his daddy's deal with the Devil.

RANDY'S DADDY

RANDY'S DADDY WAS A COAL MINER, PICKED AND CULLED FROM a long seam of mining men, none of whom knew the meaning of the word "quit."

The men had to be built that way. Coal mining was hard, dangerous work and most coal miners died far too young. From father to son, it was a heritage and a legacy that fate poured Glace Bay men into.

"A coal miner is one part owl and one part mole," Randy's daddy always told him. "From five in the morning to five at night, he spends his days in darkness rooting for coal at thirty-three cents a ton."

Thirty-three cents for every ton of coal mined. Less the cost of oil, powder, and timber. Less rent of a dollar-fifty a month. Less a doctor's fee of forty cents a month. Less a school tax of fifteen cents a month. Less a payment of thirty cents to the man who kept the tally. Less a little more for sundries and the like. Eating cost extra. It's no wonder that coal is the colour of an empty pocket.

"A coal miner is a perverse thing," Randy's daddy always told him. "A coal miner is born in the damp cave of his mother's womb, and then he starts creeping through the dank, wet darkness of the mine, picking and chipping his way down to Lord-knows-where. You'd think a man ought to know better than that."

You'd think.

"Tip your hat to the foreman, but trust the poor bare-arsed bugger who stoops and sweats at your side," Randy's daddy told him. "Trust the man who tells you where to get off when you've gone too far. Trust the man who curses in your face rather than the gentleman you must be polite to for fear of losing a living."

"Is that true?" Randy asked his daddy.

"It is a true-as-bone fact," Randy's daddy replied.

"What's a fact?" Randy asked.

"Thirty-three cents a ton, for one thing," Randy's daddy said. "A coal miner deals in facts. He has to. Because most coal miners have got themselves a family to hold onto. Why else would a man go mucking in the dirt, breathing a sniff of death with every snort he took?"

Randy shrugged an I-dunno-why kind of shrug. "Pride?" he guessed.

"Pride?" Randy's daddy laughed with a snort. "Pride only goes so far when it comes to filling an empty belly."

Which is why it probably shouldn't have surprised Randy when his daddy first told him how he had gone and sold his soul to the Devil himself.

~

RANDY'S DADDY'S DEAL

"Your granddad died a year before I was old enough to work the mine," Randy's daddy told him. "The tunnel he was working in heaved up and lay down on top of him, burying him beneath a ton or two of Cape Breton coal—which was all the grave he ever got. We buried an empty coffin in the dirt outside the churchyard. Your grandma sang 'Amazing Grace' and then she dried her eyes and just walked on."

And then Randy's daddy spat. Not being rude, you understand. The fact was, Randy's daddy had spent so many years sucking on coal dust and poverty that spitting had become just as natural as breathing. He spat black, and at forty-three, his back and shoulders had already curled over into that perpetual stoop of a question mark that passed for a spine in those parts.

"Every year we lean a little closer to the dirt," Randy's daddy told him. "Every year we dig a little deeper, looking for sunshine in the shadow of the mine. Coal is nothing more than long-dead greenings pushed down and squeezed hard; nothing but leaves and ferns that once waved beneath the sunlight glinting off of a Tyrannosaurus's backbone—fossilized sunshine and dinosaur poop. Coal is time, coal is patience, and coal is nothing more than a handful of hardened history just waiting to be dug up and burned in the belly of a woodstove."

And then he spat again.

How sweet the sound.

Randy's daddy was a deep one. It was like he spent his entire life working on a single gigantic ponder—always submerged in a sombre solitary state of reckoning—occasionally surfacing to allow his thoughts and pronouncements to drop upon Randy like slow, heavy raindrops plummeting down upon a rusted tin roof. They echoed and they splashed away, and that's all Randy really remembered about the man in later years.

The splash and the echo, fading away.

It all started on the night that Randy's daddy came home reeking of whiskey and grinning like a kid who had just discovered candy—and on a work night, to boot.

"I done it," Randy's daddy said. "I done it tonight."

"What did you do, Daddy?" Randy asked.

"I done it," Randy's daddy repeated. "I sold my soul to the Devil."

Randy stood there on the family front porch, waiting for his daddy to wink at him so that he would know that what his father was saying was nothing more than a coal-mining joke.

Only Randy's daddy didn't wink. He just stood there in the candle-lit darkness of the family front stoop.

"I met him tonight on the Hawkins Crossroad," Randy's daddy said. "He was standing there tall enough that I thought he was sitting on a ladder. A long man in a long black coat with a set of eyes that burned like a pair of lantern flies. He had the stink of brimstone about him and a fiddle cocked on his elbow and two or three imps playing at his coattails like a pack of frisky cats."

"You met your own reflection," Randy told his daddy. "You were seeing rum in your eye and nothing more." This sounded good coming out of Randy's mouth, only the more that Randy's daddy talked, the more certain Randy felt that what his daddy was telling him was the Devil's own truth.

"He told me," Randy's daddy said. "That Devil told me that he was going to bring a mine down on my head in order to steal my soul."

~

FOOLING THE FOOLER

THE WAY RANDY'S DADDY TOLD IT TO HIM, RANDY COULD SEE IT all playing out like a dream. He saw that old Devil showing his daddy how the mine was going to heave up like it did with his daddy before him, how all that gas creeping in the mine's belly was going to rise up like the fluming gorge of a fat man overstuffed. Randy saw miners screaming and darkness coming down and the preacher standing over a row of empty coffins and Momma singing "Amazing Grace."

How sweet the sound.

"But I fooled the old fooler himself," Randy's daddy told him. "I struck a deal with him."

"How did you do that?" Randy asked.

"The same as you'd deal with any man. I poked him in his vanity. I said an important man like the Devil ought not to work so hard for what could be bought easy. I told him he could have my soul outright if he'd strike me a bargain."

Randy stared at his daddy's eyes—just as dark as a shadow falling on a coal-covered face—and he could see that his daddy was telling the truth.

"So what did you ask for?" Randy said, thinking of all the sell-your-soul stories that he had ever heard. "Did you ask him for money? Did you ask for women? Did you ask for drink?"

"I asked him for none of those things," Randy's daddy said. "I asked him to help me dig."

Randy shook his head in disbelief. "Daddy," he said. "That makes about as much sense as a bucket full of hole."

"Does it?" Randy's daddy said. "It doesn't matter. I've poked a silver needle in my finger and I've signed his paper in blood smack dab at the bottom of the page. You can work alone tomorrow. From now on I'll have all the help I need."

Randy could see that there was no arguing with the man. So come the morning, Randy headed down the tunnel by himself and filled his coal cart just as best as he could. When Randy pushed the coal cart up to the mouth of the tunnel, he was surprised and amazed to see his daddy leaning on three carts crammed chock-full of the thickest slabs of coal imaginable.

By the end of the shift, Randy's daddy had hauled out over thirteen tons of coal—something like three or four men's work on a good day. Which made the company pretty happy.

By the end of the month, the boss man had begun tipping his hat at Randy's daddy instead of the other way around. And why not? Randy's daddy had paid off what he'd owed to the company store and had even begun putting some in the bank. Mind you, he still kept some in a little a pot under the bed, because Randy's daddy didn't trust a banker any farther than he could throw one.

And he still wouldn't let Randy work with him. So one fine morning, Randy stole after his daddy, keeping to the shadows as he followed him down the hole. What Randy saw down there nearly burned away his eyes.

There was the Devil himself, reaching and peeling slabs of coal just as easily as you might peel rain-soaked wallpaper. A half a dozen imps were loading the coal carts just as fast as they could.

"How deep have we got to go?" the old Devil asked.

"Deeper than this," Randy's daddy told him.

And then that Devil grumbled some, but Randy's daddy wouldn't let him stop. "Deeper," he growled.

And then Randy's daddy looked straight towards the shadow Randy was hiding in as if he could see the boy—which he could. "I see you there," Randy's daddy said. "I wondered just how long it would take before you followed me down."

"So I guess you weren't lying," Randy said.

"Did you doubt me?" Randy's daddy asked.

"Are we deep enough yet?" the Devil called out in a whiny sort of voice.

"You heard me say it yet?" Randy's daddy snapped back.

Then he turned to his son and laughed out loud. "I got it all worked out," he said. "I put it in the contract that old Slick Nick here has to keep on digging until I tell him we're down deep enough. He digs until I say so, and you know there isn't a man in these mountains who can make your daddy quit. Your daddy is a stubborn man."

Randy smiled and nodded just like his daddy expected him to, but deep down inside he wondered to himself just how stubborn the Devil was.

～

THE DEVIL'S LAST WORD

ONE MONTH LATER RANDY'S DADDY'S TUNNEL WAS CHEWING so fast that the mine had to hire out a logging mill to keep up with the timber beam and strutting. By Randy's estimate, his daddy's pet mining Devil was digging over three whole kilometres downward every day and gaining fast.

"I think he's getting homesick," Randy's daddy remarked with a grin.

Only Randy still wasn't in the grinning mood. "This is a bad business you're into," Randy told his daddy. "Hadn't you ought to be thinking about turning this deal around?"

"And what should I do?" Randy's daddy asked. "Fall down on my knees and ask that big old bearded boss man upstairs for a little slack on the line? I might as well face facts. I have cut my deal, and I'll live by it. I'll die by it too, I expect. You want to see bad business? I'll show it to you." And then he hawked up a ball of sputum about as black as the belly of a midnight burial hole.

Randy knew that dirty colour for what it was. Black lung—the stuff that turned young miners into old ones and old miners into dead ones.

"I'm dying a whole lot faster than most of us around here," Randy's daddy said. "I'll play this out until the very end."

"I guess we live as long as we're let to," Randy said. "I expect I'll walk that road myself, come a day."

"Not you," Randy's daddy said. "You're going to school."

"You know that isn't so," Randy said. "Where I'm going is back to work."

"I've made my mind up," Randy's daddy said. "You've got to leave the mine and get yourself some book learning."

"We need the money," Randy pointed out.

"For what?" Randy's daddy asked. "I have just paid the last payment on a piece of land and socked away enough bank bonds to keep your momma in good eating for the rest of her born days. And I've already put down some against your schooling."

"Daddy, you had no right to spend that money on me without my say-so," Randy said.

"Money is like water," Randy's daddy said. "It needs to be splashed around."

And that's all there was to it.

Randy argued some more, but once his momma got behind the idea, there wasn't a team of pit ponies hardy enough to pull her clear of it. So off Randy went to school, travelling all the way to Halifax. He dug into the books and found out that the black-ened print of words laid out in long, even rows was as tough a challenge as cracking into any seam of coal you care to name. But Randy stuck with it, because his daddy wanted it that way.

And all the while, Randy's daddy and his pet Devil kept working at the coal.

~

BAD NEWS

LATER THAT YEAR, RANDY HEARD THE NEWS. ONE WINTER morning the after-damp gas in his daddy's mine had built up to the point that a spark from a pick caused one of the biggest underground explosions that part of the country had ever known. It buried sixty-three men and boys. One of them was Randy's daddy.

So Randy came home on the first train, wearing a black bandana wrapped around his arm. He helped his momma hang drapings over every mirror in the house and turn the clock to the wall. The town laid out sixty-three coffins, and the preacher said his words, and Randy's momma was halfway through singing "Amazing Grace" when up walked Randy's daddy. He had his head bowed and his hat pulled down low on his forehead, looking like a man ashamed of everything he'd ever done.

"It was me," Randy's daddy told them. "I'm the cause for all this dying."

"What happened?" Randy asked.

"Well, sir, we finally got there. We dug our way clear down to Tartarus, and while Old Nick was looking around and getting an eyeload of his own stomping grounds, I leaned over and whispered something to him that I probably ought not to have."

"What'd you say to him that made him so angry?" Randy asked.

"I told him that Hell was such a pretty spot I was planning on bringing down a trainload of Cape Breton boys to plow the fire pits under and maybe grow us a whole mess of potatoes, turnips, and greens."

Randy waited for it.

"Well, I guess the thought of having to deal with that many more of me was enough to make old Nick flip his wig," Randy's daddy went on. "He stomped his cloven hooves and brought the whole kit and caboodle of the mine down upon our heads. Only the fact that I'd beaten him kept him from burying me under. But the old canker sore was still spiteful enough to make me walk all the way back home."

Randy looked up at his daddy standing there beside his own empty coffin, laughing for the joy and crying for the dead. And then Randy reached up and hugged his daddy about as hard as a man could ever hug. Momma did too, after she'd hit him a lick or so for giving her such an awful fright.

Three years later, the black lung took Randy's daddy down. But he died beneath a roof that was bought and paid for, and he didn't owe a single thin dime to the company store.

The Mark of the Fish

PORT HOOD

~

THE EARLY MI'KMAQ ORIGINALLY REFERRED TO THE AREA that is now called Port Hood as "Kek-weom-kek," a name that roughly translates to "sand bar," for its sandy low-lying beaches. Early French sailors began referring to the quiet little port area as "Justaucorps," or "up-to-one's-waistcoat," due to the port's lack of wharf. Port Hood is home to some of the warmest coastal waters in Eastern Canada. And it is on the edge of these waters where, according to legend, this next chilling story took place.

~

RING ROCK

THE OLD STORYTELLERS OF PORT HOOD SAY THAT THERE IS A large rock with a cold iron ring sunk into its side—aptly named Ring Rock—that sits nestled down close to the shoreline at the lower end of the harbour. A short distance from Ring Rock lived a family who had been blessed and cursed by the birth of two sisters, Audrey and Mabel, born eleven months apart. Audrey was the older of the two and she was as beautiful as you could imagine, with flowing blond locks and sparkling blue eyes. Mabel wasn't all that hard to look at either, but in her eyes the bedroom mirror told a totally different story.

It was the custom of this family that the children should marry by rank of birth—the oldest first and the youngest last. This rule had been all right for the girls' two older brothers, who were born twins and had married and moved away just as easily as that. But Mabel didn't care for waiting.

"My sister is so beautiful, with her long golden hair," Mabel would say. "She has her pick of the fellows and I may die an old maid if I wait for her to marry."

After a winter fever carried their mother off one lonely cold February evening, both girls decided to stay at home to take care of their father. And the girls seemed to be the best of friends. Wherever Audrey went, Mabel was sure to follow. They would do their chores together. They would walk hand in hand down at the shoreline. They would sit upon the Ring Rock and braid each other's hair, setting seashells, bright stones, and wildflowers amongst each other's long lovely locks.

People would never have guessed the fury that was buried in Mabel's heart. She always wore a sweet little smile, and she only allowed it to slip a little when she thought no one was watching her.

Shortly before Audrey's twenty-first birthday, a young man named Danny Collins came to town. He opened a small general store and on his first morning of business—Audrey's birthday—the first person to set foot in his store was none other than Audrey herself. Mabel, of course, followed closely behind her sister, but she might as well have been a candle following close behind the midday sun. Danny Collins took one look at Audrey and it was as if a giant wave had rolled into the general store and slapped him smack between the eyes.

They call it love.

A MARRIAGE PROPOSAL

BEFORE THE SUMMER WAS OUT, DANNY COLLINS HAD COME
calling to Audrey's house and asked her father if he might marry her.

"I'm not certain why you're asking *me*," Audrey's father replied.
"Seeing as it's *Audrey* you are hoping to marry."

So Danny Collins got down upon one bent knee and offered
Audrey the finest wedding ring that Port Hood had ever seen.
Audrey said yes and her father just smiled. All the while Mabel
was watching from the shadows.

Two months later, and one month before the wedding was to
take place, Mabel saw her chance. She asked Audrey to come and
sit with her at Ring Rock.

"You'll soon be married to a handsome young man," Mabel
said as they approached the rock. "This may be the last time we
ever braid each other's hair again."

Audrey laughed at that notion. "I'm getting married, it's
true," she said. "But I hardly think that will make me any less of
a sister to you."

"You might be right," Mabel replied. "But nevertheless, sit
down on the rock and let me braid your hair one last time."

And then Mabel braided Audrey's long, lovely blond hair,
twisting it tightly to the rusty iron band that was embedded into
Ring Rock.

At first, Audrey thought it was a harmless joke. Then, when
Mabel took no step towards releasing her, Audrey grew frightened. "The tide is coming in," she said. "If you don't unbraid my
hair I will drown."

"Yes," Mabel spoke at last. "You will drown and Danny Collins
will weep in sorrow and I will kiss his tears away one by one. And
sooner or later he will kiss me back and by this time next year I
will be his bride and you will be nothing but a memory."

Audrey screamed as realization sank in, but the pounding waves and the cry of the gulls masked any trace of her panic and fear. No one in town could hear her cries and Mabel only laughed as the tide crept closer.

And then Audrey grew as silent as a stone and began to hum to herself, and said something in the softest of whispers.

"What was that you said?" Mabel asked.

Audrey whispered again.

Mabel leaned close enough so that Audrey could whisper in her ear.

"All that you say is true, my sister," Audrey said. "But by the time the tide in your womb has turned, you will see seaweed and the mark of the fish." And then Audrey opened her mouth and let out an angry hiss like the sound of the wind whipping over the waves.

Mabel stepped back. She forced a laugh to try and prove that she wasn't frightened. Then she stood and watched as the tide crept up and rolled over her sister. When Audrey had stopped kicking and the bubbles had come up and out from her throat Mabel untied her sister's braid, pulled the corpse free from the iron ring, and pushed it down into the depths of the sea.

Then she went home and told her father that her sister had drowned.

～

THE MARK OF THE FISH

A GREAT STORM ROSE UP THAT NIGHT AND IT WAS NINE DAYS and nine nights before what the water had left of Audrey floated ashore. Her skin was puffy and softened by the sea. A great shroud of seaweed had tangled in her hair, a tiny crab had picked his way through, and the sea worms had already begun to work into her flesh.

And everything happened as Mabel had foreseen.

Danny Collins wept and she comforted him. In his grief he reached out for her arms as a drowning man might reach out for a freely extended hand. By the time the next summer rolled around they were married. Soon after that came the birth of their first child.

The midwife who helped deliver the child swore that the baby had been born from her mother's womb in a rush of ice cold sea water, tangled in a caul of fresh seaweed. "It had fins for feet and flippers for hands," she swore.

Whether the midwife's story was true or not is something that we will never know because that very night Mabel picked up the tiny body of her stillborn child and carried it down to the water. And when she got to the water she kept on walking.

The only trace that was ever found of Mabel was the beautiful gold wedding band that she left tied to Ring Rock by a carefully braided strand of long golden hair.

The Sight of the Stirring Curtains

DIGBY

~

THERE ARE AN AWFUL LOT OF FISHING SUPERSTITIONS IN Nova Scotia. Local fishermen will tell you that you should never turn your boat against the sun or counter-clockwise. They also believe that a piece of silver should always be placed beneath the mast of a sailing ship before she is launched, a deck hatch should never be turned completely outside down, black suitcases are considered bad luck, and whistling will bring a storm (as will throwing a penny overboard).

And some even say that the sight of seaweed on the floor and softly blowing curtains will chill a man or maid to their very soul.

~

CURTAINS, FOR CERTAIN

THERE IS A STORY THAT THEY TELL IN THE DIGBY AREA OF THE Fundy shoreline about a young girl named Jenny, a fisherman's daughter back in the days of the tall schooners. Jenny was a hard-working girl who made a living cleaning the fish that the men brought to shore. She knew the ways of the water and could tell the tide and the time with nothing more than a quick glance.

Which was all it took for her to fall head over heels in love with Big Jim Dobson. She stole one brief look at the young man while he was working on his father's boat and she knew that she and he were going to be as one.

Mind you, Jenny was nothing more than sixteen years old at the time and Jim was all of eighteen, but things happened at a different pace back in those days. Jenny married Jim that summer and the two of them moved into a small house on the seaward side of the hill, overlooking the harbour.

For a time everything was wonderful. Every morning Jenny would see Jim smiling. Every night she went to sleep listening to the steady thump of his heartbeat and the soft talking whoosh-ha-ha of the waves washing against the shoreline. Life was happy.

Then, two weeks into what looked to be a happily-ever-after marriage, the first bit of trouble set in.

"You mustn't go to sea today," Jenny told Jim.

"And why is that?" he asked.

"I saw the curtains moving last night," she said. "And there was nary a wind stirring outside."

Now every fisherman's wife in this harbour town knew that if a woman saw the curtains stirring on a windless evening that it meant there'd be a bad wind blowing the next day—a wind that might blow a loved one away. The sight of stirring curtains was what the old people would call a "forerunner," a sure and certain sign of death to come.

"Those bedroom windows are double-paned sheet glass," Jim told her. "And I caulked them myself. There is no way in the sea nor sky nor land that a smidgen of breeze could creep into this bedroom."

"Jimmy, I saw them moving," Jenny said. "It was like somebody had shackled a ghost to that curtain rod."

Jim only laughed at his young wife's fears. "Look at that sky out there," he said to her. "The air is so calm that the hay in the meadow is growing stiff from a lack of bending. There is no sign of a storm nor a bit of bad wind in the lea of a calm morning as this."

"And yet those curtains moved."

"It's calm, I tell you."

"It is calmest before a storm," Jenny warned him. "You're a fisherman, Jim. You ought to know that."

But there were fish to be caught and money to be made and a mountain of new bills that weren't going to pay themselves. So Big Jim Dobson hauled on his gumboots and clumped down to the harbour to set sail.

And Jenny stayed home to wait.

All that day the curtains continued to blow. Jenny sat and watched them. The birds outside sang sweetly. Her friends passed and called for her to join them in the outdoor sunshine. But Jenny preferred to sit there and keep her vigil, staring at those curtains.

Morning wore into afternoon and poured itself towards the evening and Jenny still kept on watching. As she watched those curtains blowing, in her mind's eye she saw the sails on Jim's schooner billowing and snapping in a high Atlantic windstorm.

The curtain rods creaked. In her mind's eye she heard the masts of a sailing ship sway. The main and fore gaff swung hard. Hawser snapped and timber groaned.

And then all at once the curtains fell to the ground like a crumpled ghost.

Jenny reached for the curtain but hesitated, her fingertips not more than an inch away from the fabric, which seemed to pucker and writhe upon the floorboards of her bedroom like a clot of jellyfish.

She reached closer.

She could smell the sea wind blowing in through the window.

Closer.

She could hear the seagulls crying in the breeze.

Closer.

She could see the shape of Jim's face, outlined in the fallen curtains. She could see him kicking against the current. She could see him trying to escape the cold and hungry Atlantic waves. She could see him opening his mouth wide into one last soul-chilling scream.

A seagull screeched just beyond the window.

Jenny sank to her knees and touched the bedroom curtains. She gasped as she found them to be sopping wet.

She wept a little while, feeling the tears spill down her cheeks, splashing on the already sodden curtains. Then she picked the curtains up, folding them carefully over her arms. She was not surprised to see the tangled clumps of fresh kelp curled beneath the fallen cotton curtains.

Later that evening they brought her Jim home to the harbour. There had been a storm and a spar had snapped and fallen upon her husband while he was bent and working. He had fallen into the sea and drowned. Only grim luck had led them to find him when they brought in a net full of fresh-caught fish and Jim's cold dead body was tangled in its weave.

Jenny was waiting on the wharf when the boat returned. The curtains, now neatly folded, hung over her arms. At least she would have a shroud to wrap him in.

Aunt Minnie's Black Cat

Cleveland

~

OME OF THE VERY BEST STORIES ARE FOUND VERY CLOSE to home. This next story was told to me by my wife, whose family passed it down to her. I have gussied and ghosted it up a bit to make it fit this collection a little snugger and hopefully have got most of the details right.

This story takes place in Cape Breton, one of the richest breeding grounds for pure tale-telling talent. I wasn't able to figure out for sure exactly where in Cape Breton this tale took place, so I have taken the liberty of setting it in Cleveland, a small community sixteen kilometres northeast of Port Hawkesbury. I apologize in advance to any in-laws who are offended by free and frequent fudging of the facts.

MEET AUNT MINNIE

It seems that Aunt Minnie was a widow, more than a handful of decades old. She lived alone in a small cottage with Mr. Coal Shadow, a sleek black cat with a bad habit of tangling Aunt Minnie's knitting.

Now, as anyone can tell you, a black cat is the worst of luck to anybody except its owner. And Mr. Coal Shadow was the very best of luck for old Aunt Minnie. He purred on her lap, kneaded her quilt with his paws every night, and never let her walk alone (that is, if she was headed in any direction that might eventually lead towards the kitchen). He glared at strangers and he managed the mouse population and he kept careful count of the birds that flew and frolicked in Aunt Minnie's rowan tree.

"Mr. Coal Shadow is my constant companion and very best friend," Aunt Minnie always said. "He sticks to me closer than my own shadow."

"How old is that cat, Aunt Minnie?" her friends and relations would ask.

"Mr. Coal Shadow is nearly as many years as I have fingers and toes," she would answer.

"You ought to be thinking about putting the old cat down," someone would invariably tell her.

"Mr. Coal Shadow will live just as long as I do and maybe just a little bit more," Aunt Minnie would answer with a sly little wink.

Then one cold winter morning Aunt Minnie walked to the kitchen and Mr. Coal Shadow did not follow beneath her feet.

"Are you sleeping, Mr. Coal Shadow?" Aunt Minnie asked.

Only Mr. Coal Shadow wasn't sleeping. The old cat was lying stretched out in Aunt Minnie's favourite rocking chair. He wasn't moving. He wasn't stirring.

The poor old cat had died.

"Well," Aunt Minnie said. "There is only one thing to do for this cat."

And so, in the heart of a very cold Cape Breton winter, Aunt Minnie went out to the back shed and got her best gardening shovel. She carried Mr. Coal Shadow to the foot of his favourite bird-watching tree, the big old rowan—which some folks call witch elm and some folks call mountain ash—and she began to dig a hole.

It was awfully hard work. The ground was frozen as hard as a tax collector's heart. Roots tangled around the shovel blade and gave her grief.

When the snow started falling it made things worse. It was a soft-looking snow, the kind that some people call pretty. But looking at a pretty snowfall and standing out there ankle deep in the cold wet stuff are two completely different things. Aunt Minnie knew that it was several kinds of foolish to keep digging out here with the snow piling up the way it was—but she also knew that there was no way at all that she was going to leave her poor cat without a decent burial.

By the time Aunt Minnie had finished digging the grave, the snow had nearly covered Mr. Coal Shadow. She scooped him up and whispered something in his ear, and then she placed Mr. Coal Shadow in the grave, wrapped in the shroud of his favourite green plaid kitty blanket. She put his catnip mouse and his dish in the grave with him. Then she sang three hymns, shivering a little with the cold, before she finally buried the cat once and for all.

She walked back to her front door slowly, leaning on the shovel like it was a crutch. The tears had icicled her eye lashes up so that she could hardly see, but she knew her way just the same.

She tapped on her door as if she were coming to somebody's house for tea. Then she went inside and put the big iron kettle on the stove and sat down in her rocking chair to wait.

Only she had worked herself far too hard. The kettle had just started to whistle when death's cold hand reached out and stilled Aunt Minnie's heart.

The kettle had whistled itself dry by the time Aunt Minnie's niece tapped on the door and let herself in. When she stepped into the kitchen, she saw her Aunt Minnie sitting in her rocking chair with a shawl about her shoulders and a quilt upon her lap. And upon the quilt was the old black cat.

The old cat purred contentedly.

"Well at least she didn't die alone," her niece said.

When she looked again the cat was gone.

The Haunting of Esther Cox

AMHERST

~

IN THE BUSTLING CUMBERLAND COUNTY TOWN OF Amherst, back in the late nineteenth century a tale of terror unfolded—a tale so terrible that it is remembered to this very day. This story has been told and retold in volumes of ghostly folklore and newspaper articles across the continent. It is so well loved and wholly feared that it has been immortalized in the streets of Amherst with a gigantic two-storey mural painted by well-known Nova Scotia artists Susan Tooke and Richard Rudnicki.

The story is known as the Great Amherst Mystery, and it pertains to the haunting of one Esther Cox.

~

ESTHER'S EARLY LIFE

ESTHER WAS BORN IN THE TOWN OF UPPER STEWIACKE. HER mother died three weeks after her birth, due to complications from the labour. At birth Esther weighed a mere five pounds. Soon after she was born, Esther's father, Archibald T. Cox, remarried and moved to Maine with his new family, leaving Esther and her older sister, Jane, in the care of their grandmother.

By 1848, Esther's grandmother had died, and she and Jane were living in a crowded two-storey house on Princess Street in Amherst, Nova Scotia. The bills were primarily paid by the girls' uncle, Daniel Teed, a foreman in the Amherst Shoe Factory. In addition to Uncle Daniel and Esther and Jane, the house also sheltered Daniel's wife, Olive, and their two sons, five-year-old Willie and one-year-old George.

Esther was short and rather stout. Her eyes were grey with flecks of blue. Her hair was a curly dark brown and she wore it short to allow for easy maintenance. Esther was quiet and fairly helpful and prone to daydreaming. Her demeanour was pleasant and she was quite popular with the local youth.

However, at the age of eighteen Esther Cox's life became pure hell.

~

THE TROUBLE BEGINS

THE TROUBLE FIRST STARTED ONE NIGHT IN EARLY SEPTEMBER, when Esther awakened Jane in the bed that they shared.

"There are mice in the bed," Esther said. "I can hear them scratching."

Jane listened carefully, only to discover that the scratching noises weren't actually coming from the bed itself, but rather from beneath it.

"It's the box of quilt makings under the bed," Jane said. "I bet you anything those mice are building a nest in it."

The two of them gingerly slid the old cardboard dress box crammed full of quilting patches out from beneath their bed and into the middle of the floor.

"Open it," Jane said.

"You first," Esther replied.

All at once the box lid flew open and quilt patches began to flutter about the room like tiny flying carpets. The box bounced repeatedly as if someone were slamming it upon the floorboards. At the same time, the quilt flew from the bed and draped itself over Jane and Esther's heads. Every time they pulled the quilt off, it folded itself back over their heads as if someone were shaking and draping it in midair.

At this point Uncle Daniel rushed into the room. "What's wrong?" he asked.

By this time the disturbance had completely subsided. All that Uncle Daniel could see was a pair of young girls sitting on their bedroom floor with the bed quilt tented over their heads.

"Some of us need to work in the morning," he grumbled, going back to his bedroom with a rueful chuckle. He was a good man and did his best to see the funny things in life.

Only it wasn't so funny later that evening when the sound of Esther's panic-stricken screams woke the entire household.

"I'm dying!" she shrieked. "I'm dying!"

Jane leaped from the bed as the family rushed in. They all stared at Esther in absolute terror. Esther's hair stood straight out as if she had been struck by lightning. Her skin was blotched the colour of blood. Her flesh began to bloat and swell and she could barely manage to catch her breath.

"I'm dying," she repeated.

"It's a fever," her uncle decided.

Only it was no mere fever. A fever wouldn't explain all the noise and commotion. Loud raps and bangs echoed through the room as if someone were beating on the walls from the inside with a massive hammer. The quilt again began to turn itself over as if some invisible hand was trying its hardest to unmake the bed.

The family watched in horror until morning, when the event culminated in what sounded like a loud clap of thunder, right in the bedroom. It left behind a stench of something like sulphur. The odd noises finally subsided, the quilt ceased its antics, and Esther regained her normal health. She caught her breath, the unwholesome bloating of her limbs and flesh seemed to pass, and her skin resumed its normal pigmentation. For a moment, all was calm.

~

A MESSAGE FROM BEYOND

As THE DAYS WENT ON, ESTHER'S HEALTH SEEMED TO WORSEN. The nightly visitations continued. The banging and thumping that tormented her grew bolder.

Finally, four days later, a doctor was summoned to Esther's room. He might have been called earlier, but ready cash was hard to come by in those days and doctors cost a lot of money. "She's clammy and sweating," the doctor said. "But she doesn't seem to have much in the way of a fever."

He sounded a little impatient. He had listened to the family's story and privately considered it to be nothing more than foolish ranting. Still, he was a doctor and he was honour-bound to do his best to help the poor girl.

As he continued his examination, the strange banging sound began to echo through the room. There was also a scratching noise that sounded as if someone were working a very sharp set of nails across a blackboard.

"Look," Uncle Daniel said, pointing up at a spot on the wall just above Esther's headboard. Words were beginning to emerge on the wall, as if someone were scratching them out from beneath the plaster. The group watched in cold terror as the message began to emerge:

ESTHER COX, YOU ARE MINE TO KILL.

THE SITUATION WORSENS

OVER THE NEXT FOUR MONTHS THE CONDITIONS GREW WORSE. The hammering noises began to move throughout the household. At one point it sounded as if a 150-pound man were jumping upon the roof. Another time Uncle Daniel's wife stared in amazement and terror as a barrel of potatoes was flung around the house's basement. The potatoes rolled and chased her about the cellar.

In December of that year, Esther, worn down by her continuing nightly ordeal, was struck with a severe case of diphtheria. She was bedridden for two solid weeks and the family enjoyed two weeks of uninterrupted rest. The diphtheria seemed to ward off the paranormal activity.

Following her recovery, Esther journeyed to Sackville, New Brunswick, to stay with a married aunt. No episodes of paranormal activity were reported in the Sackville residence.

However, in January, when Esther returned to Amherst, things resumed with a vengeance. Along with the banging and the scratching and the moving furniture, lit matches began to materialize in mid-air, usually just below ceiling level. As they materialized they dropped to the floor, still lit. The matter became even more serious when Esther reported hearing voices whispering to her that the house would burn down to the ground before the month was over.

The family had to face facts. Esther had to go.

The Whites, a neighbouring couple who needed an extra set of hands around their farm, took Esther in but had to return her after tools began flying around wherever she went. Even the local Baptist church could provide no peace for poor Esther, as the mysterious pounding and scratching followed her even into those sacred walls.

Esther was losing hope. Something had to be done—and fast.

WHO YOU GONNA CALL?

In March 1878, Esther was invited to stay at the Saint John, New Brunswick, home of Captain James Beck—a man with a keen interest in the paranormal. In addition to Captain Beck, several scientists, a handful of amateur occultists and investigators of unearthly phenomena, and a trio of local clergymen were invited along on a sort of nineteenth century "ghost-busting" operation.

The team studied Esther for some time. She would sit on a wooden chair secured to a thick rug, eliminating any possibility of her making the banging sound with the legs of the chair. The rapping and banging continued in spite of the precautionary carpet. A pot of water was placed beside the rug. The water immediately began to boil, in spite of the fact that there was no fire anywhere close to the pot.

By now Esther was comfortable conversing with the banging spirits. The spirits, if spirits they were, would answer onlooker's questions. If someone asked, "How old am I?" the spirits would bang out the proper number. She knew the names and personalities of each of the spirits that haunted her. Above all else, Esther maintained that any vandalism or misdoings were strictly the fault of the spirits.

"None of it is my doing," she swore. "The spirits are doing it all."

Shortly after she arrived at Captain Beck's home, Esther met Walter Hubbell, an American actor on tour through the Maritimes. Hubbell saw opportunity in Esther's sad plight, and convinced her to let him study her further in her own home.

Hubbell became quite close with Esther and her family. Uncle Daniel and Aunt Olive were quite taken with the dashing young actor and he won both the trust and the heart of young Esther Cox. However, the spirits who haunted Esther seemed less than fond of Hubbell. In fact, whenever Hubbell entered Esther's bedroom, furniture would begin to shift wildly and objects he was holding would be jerked from his hands. Once a large butcher knife flew at him, barely missing his throat.

In June 1879, Hubbell convinced Esther to accompany him on a theatrical tour. He won Uncle Daniel and Aunt Olive over with his talk of how much money they were going to make for Esther.

Hubbell booked Esther in at theatres all over the Maritimes so the public could come witness the paranormal phenomenon with their own eyes. However, their first performance, in Pictou, was a total bust. Esther's spirits suffered from stage fright—she sat there on her chair but nothing happened. In the end people began throwing objects at the stage. They booed loudly and shouted, "Fake! Fake!" A riot broke out and the theatre was nearly destroyed. Esther's all-too-short theatrical career came to a crashing halt then and there.

After that, Hubbell and Esther had a falling out. Hubbell went on to write and publish a short dissertation entitled "The Great Amherst Mystery"—a book that was quite successful and made him an awful lot of money. Surprisingly enough, Esther didn't see any of the resulting profits.

THE STORY CONTINUES

AFTER HUBBELL'S ABRUPT DEPARTURE, ESTHER MANAGED TO find sanctuary in the home of a local farmer named Arthur Davis—a man who was certain that he could learn to put up with the banging, the moaning, and the occasional moving furniture. However, Davis could not put up with having his barn burn down, which is exactly what happened a short time after Esther moved in. Arthur Davis was not inclined to write the barn-burning off as the work of spirits. Instead, he charged Esther with arson.

Esther was tried and convicted and sentenced to four months in jail. However, the townsfolk felt sorry for Esther's situation and convinced local authorities to release her after she had served only a single month of jail time. No disturbances were reported while she was serving her jail sentence.

After her release from jail, Esther was taken in by yet another household, the Van Amburghs. There, she lived in mostly untroubled peace. She found her strength through continual prayer and read the Holy Bible every day. She was still plagued by the occasional spirit—pieces of furniture sometimes slid and moved and her bedding would periodically fly off her bed—but none of the events were as frequent or powerful as before. Things had begun to look up for the girl.

In time Esther fell in love and married one Mr. Adams of Springdale, Nova Scotia. She outlived Adams and was then married a second time, to a Mr. Shanahan of Brockton, Massachusetts.

For whatever reason, the mysterious events seemed to settle as she grew into her life. There were still occasional outbursts of activity, but nothing to the extent of her years in Amherst.

Esther Cox Shanahan died peacefully in 1912 at the age of 52. The house on Princess Street still stands to this very day.

The Broken Heart

LUNENBURG

~

THE NEW LUNENBURG ACADEMY WAS FIRST OPENED ON November 7, 1895. It was built to replace the original academy, which had been located at the heart of the town but was destroyed by a chimney flue fire in 1893. The ground floor of the new academy building contained six large classrooms with separate cloakrooms for boys and girls. The second floor held six more classrooms, an equal number of cloakrooms, a laboratory, and a library. There was a large assembly hall on the third floor, capable of seating over four hundred individuals. The ceilings throughout the building were of white wood and were beautifully panelled. The floors and wainscotting were of white birch while the rest of the interior was finished in a mixture of ash and birch. Four towers adorned the building. In one of these towers hung a large bell, which weighed over six hundred pounds and which was cast at the Lunenburg Iron Company.

According to the *Educational Review* of February 1896, the new Lunenburg Academy "occupied one of the finest and most commanding sites in the Province, being visible for many miles around." The hill that the academy stood upon was originally known as Gallows Hill because it was where hangings were performed throughout the early years of Lunenburg's history.

There are a great many ghost stories surrounding the Lunenberg Academy. Some people say that the ghost of a retired teacher keeps watch on the school from an eerie spectral rocking chair, and they claim that you can hear her rocking chair squeaking and creaking on certain nights of the year. There has also been talk of a ghost that lurks in the basement washroom, but as of yet these rumours remain unsubstantiated. Others swear that the ghost of Peter Mailman, a convicted wife-murderer and the last man to be hung on Gallows Hill, still walks this area. Some folks claim that they have seen his ghost in the old berry-picking ground, still carrying the axe that he used to slay his loving wife.

It is natural to hear such stories concerning such a very old building as the academy, but the school's location likely also plays a part in its paranormal popularity. Surrounding the academy on three sides is the Hillcrest Cemetery, the second-oldest cemetery in the area, with grave markers dating back as far as 1761.

A stone's throw from the academy stands the gravestone of Sophia L. McLachlan. It is here, in the shadow of the Lunenburg Academy, high atop Gallows Hill, that we find Lunenburg's most intriguing ghost story, a fascinating tale of false accusation and bitter mortal grief.

~

A FATAL BROKEN HEART

SOPHIA HAD CERTAINLY SEEN HER SHARE OF HARDSHIP. HER father, Joseph, and her grandfather, Benjamin, made a modest living building dories and whalers. Sophia's father's income was eaten up by the demands of his large family, which also included his wife, Lavinia, and Sophia's five younger sisters: Elizabeth,

Eldora, Ella May, Luthia, and Atholea. The entire family lived in a small rented cottage on Pelham Street, just a short distance from Joseph's family home.

On October 12, 1878, tragedy struck the family when six-year-old Ella May died of scarlet fever. Two days later, the fever took three-year-old Atholea as well. At thirteen years of age, Sophia was devastated by the family loss. As the oldest child, she had given freely of herself, spending many long hours taking care of her sisters. At this point she felt as much like a mother as a sister could.

Sophia helped out her family the only way she knew how, taking a position as an apprentice to a well-known local dressmaker by the name of Anne Trask. Mrs. Trask was a single woman raising two children, thirteen-year-old Charles and eleven-year-old Nellie.

Sophia was a hard-working girl and she proved herself to be both capable and industrious. Above all else, Sophia was trustworthy. Mrs. Trask came to count heavily on her to take care of the shop whenever she found the need to run errands around the town. It was after one such excursion, however, that Mrs. Trask came back to the shop to find ten dollars missing from the cash drawer.

Back in 1879, ten dollars was a significant sum of money for anyone to mislay, and Mrs. Trask was furious about it. She turned on Sophia and blamed her for the loss of the money. "You stole it," she accused. "There's no use in denying it. You were the only one here who could have done it."

Sophia swore she was innocent, but Mrs. Trask was deaf to her protestations. She fired Sophia and sent her home in tears.

Things did not improve at home. When Sophia told her parents about the incident, they were furious. Lavinia felt that the family had been humiliated by the shame of Sophia's larceny. Joseph was worried that the blot on his family's reputation might prove bad for his boat-building business.

To make matters worse, Mrs. Trask made good and certain that the entire town knew about the theft. Sophia's friends shunned her. Her neighbours gossiped about her.

So there Sophia was, a fourteen-and-a-half-year-old girl with absolutely no one to turn to. Every day, she would trudge sadly up Gallows Hill, cast herself down upon the graves of her two younger sisters, and weep into the muddy rain-soaked grass. She would weep the entire day away and sometimes she would stay all night, regardless of the weather. Meanwhile, Mrs. Trask declared that if Sophia did not return the ten dollars that had been stolen, then she would have no other alternative than to go to the sheriff.

But tragedy arrived before the sheriff did.

Sophia became weaker by the day. Soon she was too weak to make the long walk to the graveyard. Instead she stayed at home in her bedroom. She read her Bible and prayed continuously.

Lavinia soon forgot about the shame of the incident and began worrying about her daughter's health instead. After losing two daughters to the fever, she couldn't bear the thought of losing another.

Sophia told her mother that she should not worry. "I will soon be with my beloved little sisters," she said. "And my innocence will be known by everyone."

Her mother protested, feeling badly that she had treated her daughter so cruelly.

"Don't apologize," Sophia said. "There is no need. I feel easy now and happy and completely at peace."

Later that day, Sophia wrote a long letter to Mrs. Trask, telling the woman of her feelings and pleading her innocence. And shortly thereafter, on September 19, 1879, Sophia L. McLachlan died peacefully.

Sophia's death, coming so soon after the scandal of the theft, triggered an immediate public uproar. How had such a tragic event come to be? Was it murder? Was it suicide? The doctor, prompted by local authorities, called for an immediate inquest.

A coroner's jury met that afternoon. After due consideration, the jury reached a unanimous decision: "Death occurred as a result of paralysis of the heart brought on by extreme agitation caused by peculiar circumstances."

In short, Sophia McLachlan had died of a broken heart.

Sophia was buried in Hillcrest Cemetery three days later. Her grave was marked with a crude wooden cross constructed by her father. A week following her burial, thirteen-year-old Charles Trask confessed to stealing the ten dollars in question. He had hidden the money beneath his mattress, afraid to spend it and afraid to confess to stealing it.

Tearfully, Mrs. Trask read Sophia's last letter over the young girl's grave (this is that letter, word for word):

> Dear Mrs. Trask,
>
> It is now just half past nine o'clock and I am sitting down to write you a few lines, and doing it to remind you of what you have accused me, so innocent, for you blamed me for stealing your money but there is One above who knows that I did not take it.
>
> Nothing would tempt me to do so.
>
> Mrs. Trask, you will cause my death, and it is a fearful thing. It can't be concealed forever. It will come out some day and then what will your feelings be?
>
> You know that if you have any fear of God that it is awful to be blamed if you are innocent. I was writing this letter when you was down. I was never brought in a scrap like this in my life. You will never have me to blame again. I am nearly gone; my hand trembles so that I can scarcely write. There will be many a long hour that you will think of this, if you have any heart at all. I would not take a false oath, but I did not take your money. You know it is a fearful thing to lie. What it is ever in this world, it is in the next.
>
> Mrs. Trask, take the Bible and turn to the XX Chapter of Exodus and tell Charles to read the 16th verse of it for my sake. You also take Matthew Chapters V, VI and VII; read them; see if there are not

verses that will answer this. For example, take the 1st verse of the VII, and the 10th, 11th and 12th verses of the V Chapters.

Mrs. Trask, you know that when I am gone they can say what they like; but of what they say I am innocent of, and I am not afraid to fear death. I know a secret but I ain't going to say anything about it, but I won't say that I will never tell you.

I can't write anymore.
From your friend,
Sophie L. McLachlan

PS: When you hear that song, "My grave, my grave, keep green," think of me! Mrs. Trask, you have to make it out the best way you can. Think how this will disgrace my father, mother, and sisters and all belonging to me, but you brought it on. Good bye for ever! No one knows I wrote you this letter. You can tell my people about it when I am gone.

Shortly after the funeral, the citizens of Lunenburg collectively donated enough money to erect a proper tombstone on Sophia's grave. The tombstone's inscription reads as follows:

ERECTED BY SYMPATHISING FRIENDS
IN MEMORY OF
SOPHIA L.
DAUGHTER OF JOSEPH AND LAVINIA MCLACHLAN
WHO DIED SUDDENLY
SEPTEMBER 19TH, 1879
AGED 14 YRS 6 MONTHS

———————

FALSELY ACCUSED
SHE DIES OF A BROKEN HEART
BEFORE HER DEATH SHE REFERRED HER ACCUSER
TO THE FOLLOWING TEXTS OF SCRIPTURE

Below this line were the scripture references that Sophia listed in her letter.

The tombstone stood where the citizens of Lunenburg had set it for over a century. As time went by, erosion almost completely wore away what was written there. Soon the inscription and the story attached to it was lost for all time.

But in 1986, the Bluenose General Radio Service Society of Lunenburg decided to repair Sophia's gravesite and do something to make it more noticeable. The town of Lunenburg, still nursing the ache in its collective conscience, promised to help the GRS Society out in any way possible. Shortly thereafter, the GRS commissioned a local ironworker to construct a decorative iron fence and railing to set Sophia's grave apart from all of the other tombstones in the cemetery—in spite of the Cemetery Commission's bylaw strictly forbidding the placement of such fences.

Now, thanks to the GRS Society and the citizens of Lunenberg, Sophia's grave has been restored. Along with the new iron railing, which makes it easy to spot the gravesite from a distance, there are two decorative plaques that retell Sophia's story. Each plaque is attached to a chain, and the chains are suspended from an iron heart, broken in the middle. The biblical quotes that Sophia refers to in her letter to Mrs. Trask are reproduced on one of the wrought iron plaques.

> Exodus XX, 16: Thou shalt not bear false witness against thy neighbour.
>
> Matthew V, 10: Blessed are they which are persecuted for righteousness' sake; for theirs is the kingdom of Heaven.
>
> Matthew V, 11: Blessed are ye, when men shall revile you, and persecute you, and shall say all manner of evil against you falsely, for my sake.

Matthew V, 12: Rejoice, and be exceedingly glad; for
   great is your reward in Heaven: for so persecuted
   they the prophets which were before you.
Matthew VII, 1: Judge not, that ye be not judged.

Some people swear that on certain nights they can hear the
sound of Sophia weeping at her gravesite. It may just be the wind
working through the tombstones. It may just be the calling of
some gentle little night bird. Whatever the cause, do not grieve,
for there is a happy side to this story as well: just as many times as
the weeping has been reported, folks have also reported that the
figures of three young girls—Sophia, Ella May, and Atholea—have
been seen running and giggling through the thick Lunenburg
mist. May they always be happy and may they play together forever
in the green grass of the Hillcrest Cemetery.

The Lunenburg Werewolf

LUNENBURG

~

WEREWOLVES HAVE ALWAYS BEEN ONE OF MY FAVOURITE movie monsters. I have always felt them to be both tragic and terrifying.

So when I found out that an actual werewolf was reported to have lived in the little town of Lunenburg, I knew I needed to include it here. Let me tell you about Gallows Hill, and the cemetery that some people swear is the burial place of Hans Gerhardt—the werewolf of Lunenburg.

~

NANNETTE IN THE WILDERNESS

IT WAS LATE DECEMBER 1755—A TIME OF ALL-TOO-REAL horror, shortly after the Acadian Expulsion had taken place. The Acadians had been brutally rounded up and ruthlessly removed from their homes around the Maritimes. Barns and farmhouses had been burned down or simply taken over. Homesteads had been given over to anyone who was not remotely French Acadian. Only a few courageous and desperate families had remained, hiding in the woods and wilderness, living in caves like animals.

In the turmoil a young Nova Scotia Acadian girl by the name of Nannette had become separated from her family. She'd lived for a time by herself in the woodlands. She'd learned to hunt and to forage and had managed to survive. Her life had changed and she'd done her very best to adapt to this change. After a while of wandering she'd fallen in with a band of Mi'kmaq, who'd treated her as one of their own.

Now Nannette accompanied her Mi'kmaq friends into a small German settlement on the outskirts of Lunenburg. They'd come to trade for steel utensils and spices that were hard to find. It was there that Wilhelmina Buchart spotted Nannette.

"That girl," Wilhelmina said. "She is a white girl. She should stay here."

The Mi'kmaq were cautious at first. They had been taken advantage of more than once by the settlers and were feeling somewhat protective of the little girl. Still, Wilhelmina's argument had some sense to it. The girl belonged with her people and the winter was coming on and food was beginning to grow scarce.

A deal was struck. Nannette did not have any say in her fate. She was still very young, and a little shy at that. She did not ask why the woman was giving so many supplies to her Mi'kmaq friends. She did not wonder when they told her to stay here awhile. She did not question the Mi'kmaq when they told her that they might be back in the summertime.

Nannette's life changed again.

And again she would have to learn to adapt.

HANS GERHARDT

Nannette grew into a woman and became known as one of the town beauties. More than a few young fellows were intrigued at the notion of a woman who had lived such an exciting life. The thought of marrying someone who knew how to hunt and fish and live out of doors was exciting to these young country boys.

The man who eventually won Nannette's heart was Hans Gerhardt, a strong, sturdy Germen lad with a reputation for a ready smile—filled with strong white teeth—and a surprisingly quick temper.

For a time it seemed as if Hans truly loved Nannette. They worked hard on their farm and he was constantly at her side, almost overprotective in his attachment to her. By all appearances the two seemed to be a happy couple and a wonderful part of a growing town.

After their first year of marriage, Nannette gave birth to a baby daughter. The child seemed to bring out the she-wolf in Nannette. She was fiercely devoted to the little girl, whom she called Marie. But the closer Nannette grew to little Marie, the more Hans distanced himself from Nannette. He seemed to brood and recede into the shadows of their life together. His hatred and jealousy of Marie grew almost palpably.

Strangely, Nannette never noticed. Perhaps growing up alone as she did had handicapped her social radar. Whatever the reason, she did not pick up on the intensity of Hans's hated for their young daughter.

Hans began sleeping alone in the kitchen, rather than in their marriage bed. He spent more and more time in the woods. When Nannette asked him what he did out there, he would smile at her with his strong white teeth and reply with a short retort: "Hunting."

When Hans would seethe and growl at their daughter, Nannette would blame it on his working too hard. She feared that he was making himself sick and did not think to suspect any ill-feeling. Even when he would snatch up his red hunting hat with a curse and stalk off into the darkness with a growl on his lips, Nannette seemed none the wiser.

Still, she had begun to worry. How, she wondered, could a man be so jealous of a little child? What sort of an animal would let that feeling take hold within him?

She would soon find out.

~

A BEAST IN THE NIGHT

It was about this time that local farmers began to complain about a mysterious beast that was prowling the outskirts of the settlement late at night. It was a strangely shaped creature that followed night travellers far too closely in a swift and stealthy stalking motion. It sometimes stood upright and sometimes galloped on all fours. Sometimes the beast was seen at the window of a cottage—a pair of savage eyes gazing in from the darkness beyond.

"It is a bear, perhaps," some farmers suggested. "Or a kind of wolf."

But the older men who had seen a little more of life began to wonder just exactly what sort of beast this was. They spoke of an ancient legend concerning a man who had swallowed a wolf. Whatever the man would eat, the wolf would too. Then, when the wolf grew large and powerful, it would burst free from the man's skin, drawn out by the swelling of the full moon.

The younger men laughed and told them to go back to their knitting. But old men know an awful lot.

Livestock began to go missing. Lambs and sheep and goats and cattle were found with their throats torn open and the blood drained from their carcasses. Traps were set and hunting parties went out frequently with dogs and muskets. But to no avail. Whatever was out there knew how to stay hidden.

~

THE BEAST BREAKS FREE

IN THE LATE SUMMER, TRAGEDY STRUCK. IT WAS BERRY SEASON. The woodlands were covered with luscious wild blueberries. Hans took a large basket out to pick, and Nannette stayed at home to rock little Marie to sleep on the kitchen settee. When the child was sleeping comfortably, Nannette tucked her tight in her cradle and, picking up a basket of her own, decided to join Hans in the far woods.

"Where is the baby?" Hans asked.

"Asleep in the house," she told him.

That knowledge seemed to spark Hans into great speed. His powerful fingers tore at the blueberry bushes, snatching berries as quickly as could be imagined. Nannette told herself that he must be worried about leaving their daughter alone in the cabin and that this sudden haste was a good sign. Perhaps she had been wrong in mistrusting his feelings. Perhaps he really loved their daughter.

When Hans's basket was full, he stood and turned. Nannette stood as well. "No," he said, with a grin of his big white teeth. "Stay here and fill your basket. Later you can make us a pie. I will take my basket home, empty it, and return."

"Will you see to Marie?" Nannette asked hopefully.

"I will see to the child," Hans answered. And then he showed her his big white teeth a final time before turning his back on her and walking towards the cabin.

Nannette continued to pick. It was good to be out here all by herself. Even the most doting mother grows a little weary tending constantly to the needs of a baby. Still, she began to worry. What could be keeping Hans? She told herself that he might be cooking supper. She told herself that he might be taking a nap. She told herself that he might be taking care of little Marie.

She thought of his big white teeth, of a smile that was almost too large and too hungry for a man's mouth. And then she turned and ran for the house.

When she got there, she found no trace of life. The baby was gone and so was her husband. She looked about as much as she could before racing to a neighbouring farm, where she gasped out her story to a group of local farmhands.

The men sprang into action, searching the house and fields for the child. They found Hans deep in the forest, beside a low gurgling brook. He sprang up at them with a fierce snarling cry, snapping at their throats and exposed hands.

"He seemed more beast than man," one witness said.

After they managed to tie him up, they found what was left of Marie.

~

A SAVAGE END

HANS WAS LOCKED IN THE LUNENBURG JAIL. HE SPENT THE first night howling and baying like a caged wolf. The full moon, welling up over the town of Lunenburg, served only to infuriate this caged beast man. The town jailer feared for his own life.

On the next afternoon the town officials met and decided Hans Gerhardt's fate. It took very little time for the judge and jury to come to a decision. Hans Gerhardt was sentenced to be hanged.

But the execution was doomed to failure. The next morning when the jailer opened the jailhouse door, he was horrified to find Hans lying in a pool of his own blood on the floor of the jail cell. Hans had used his strong white teeth to tear open the veins in both of his arms. The Lunenburg werewolf had met his final end.

The Capstick Bigfoot

CAPSTICK

~

YOU WILL FIND THE TOWN OF CAPSTICK, ORIGINALLY known as Wreck Cove, on one of the most northern points of Cape Breton, just a few kilometres shy of Meat Cove. Capstick is a green place, with welcoming waters and a cove that is bordered by high, steep cliffs. If you stand on those cliffs and keep a sharp eye seaward, you may even spot a pod of whales swimming in the water. And if you keep an even sharper eye towards the forest and hills, you might catch yourself a peek of the Capstick Bigfoot.

~

BIG EARS AND BIG FEET

OVER THE LAST CENTURY THERE HAVE BEEN MANY REPORTED sightings of a gigantic humanoid with long shaggy fur in the forests around Capstick. The Mi'kmaq even have a word for this beast—they call it "Se'skwetew," which literally translates to "one who screams loudly."

The Capstick Bigfoot has been described as an eight-foot-tall ape-like beast with long dangling arms that reach to his kneecaps, a tangle of snarled dirty hair, large brown soulful eyes, and a pair of long ears that stick out from his head like open car doors. Local storytellers say that the beast has been spotted off and on in these parts ever since the coal mines began blasting and drilling in the area.

Did early miners unintentionally wake something from a deep prehistoric subterranean hibernation? Are those long car-door ears sensitive to the loud blasting? In any case, an awful lot of people have seen the Capstick Bigfoot over the years. Several have nearly run it over while driving their vehicles. Others have complained about losing their hunting spoils to it.

"I had a big buck winched up in a tree," one old hunter claimed. "We had it way out on the end of a sturdy limb, tied and wrapped in an old bedsheet to keep the horseflies from off the meat. My buddy was going to bring his four-wheeler around to help haul the carcass home but the next morning when we got there the deer was gone. The winch was there, each knot untangled. There was no way a bear could have done something like that. There was also no way anybody else would have stumbled across that deer carcass, hung that high. No, sir, it was something else that took that meat."

Rabbit snares have been emptied and camp coolers cleaned out. Some of these occurrences should likely be blamed on bears and raccoons. Some of them should be blamed on vandals and thieves. But the fact is it takes an awful lot to feed a full-grown Bigfoot.

Even so, hunters who have encountered the Capstick Bigfoot have not felt the need to shoot it. One look at those soulful brown eyes is usually enough to discourage them from taking the shot. By all reports, the beast's gaze looks far too human for anyone to have the heart to shoot him.

Other local folk will tell you how the Capstick Bigfoot has helped them out in times of trouble. One man reported having a

stuck truck pushed out of a muddy spot by a gigantic furry creature. Another camper swears that the *Se'skwetew* stacked up a large
load of firewood for him as a favour.

So far there have no reports of the Capstick Bigfoot actually
attacking anyone. It will come up behind a hunter or stand beside
a roadway, but mostly it just seems to be watching.

According to recent sources, the beast has not been spotted in
the Capstick area since the early 1990s, but the fact is the terri-
tory around these little coastal towns is still thick and primordi-
ally overgrown, and there could very easily be an entire family of
these creatures still prowling the woods for forgotten coolers and
"guddling" the rivers for trout. At least, that's what Clancy would
have you believe...

~

CLANCY SEES THE CAPSTICK BIGFOOT

CLANCY WAS HUNGRY AND ONLY A TROUT WOULD DO.

Back then, if a Highlander like Clancy wanted a trout, he
didn't go looking for any hook or fishing pole. You see, the
Highlanders had themselves a trick for catching trout, more
surefire and certain than any bait or lure you care to mention.
And Clancy, even though he was born and raised in Capstick,
was Highland to the bone. So Clancy knew just how to "guddle" a
trout, as the Highlanders called it.

To successfully guddle a trout, or any other fish you care to
mention, you first have to learn how to think like a trout, which
is a pretty easy trick to accomplish because most fish don't *think*,
they just *need*. Just like any other living thing, a fish has certain
undeniable needs that go a little beyond merely wanting. A fish
needs food to eat. A fish needs shade to keep cool. A fish needs
something to hide under to stay safe.

Clancy knew that all he had to do was find those three things and he'd be able to guddle himself a fish. So first he found himself a leafy birch tree leaning over a cool running brook. The leaves of the tree gave shade and the bugs that crawled and fell off of the leaves offered a good supply of fish food. Next Clancy knelt down on the rock ledge beneath the tree. The rock was a perfect thing for the fish to take shelter under to hide from predators.

Then Clancy leaned down and let his arm slip into the cold stream water. He kept still, thinking cool, calm tree-thoughts. Before too long, Clancy, in his mind, was nothing but a big old willow tree leaning down over a cool running stream.

He let his fingers hang and dangle. Then, when he felt something moving, he hooked his fingers slowly up underneath the rock. This was always a dangerous part of the procedure—you never knew when there might be a big old snapping turtle down there under the rock instead of the trout you were looking for.

Clancy let his fingers move and waver in the water like a fistful of weeds. He felt something skitter across his palm. It might have been a frog or a big old water bug. It might have been a root. It might have been a long skinny string of water weeds. It might even have been a streak of rock. But Clancy knew full well that what he was feeling wasn't anything else but the tail of a fish.

He hoped it was a trout. It might have been a pickerel or a stickleback perch. He wouldn't know for sure until he had it up on dry land.

He reached up his fingers, just a little, and he stroked the belly of the fish. It wriggled, enjoying the petting sensation. Clancy continued to let his fingers glide and stroke along the fish's belly, moving upwards until he could feel the fringed hinge of the fish's gill.

He was so close he could taste the trout. With one quick flick he had the fish's gills snagged around his fingers. He raised the fish up out of the water, keeping his fingers hooked in as deeply as possible. The fish flapped and twisted, trying to break free, but Clancy brought its head down against the rock with a bang, knocking it stupid.

Clancy looked down at the fish and grinned so wide his teeth hurt. He had caught himself a fine fat trout and that would be dinner.

He was still grinning when he noticed how dark it had suddenly got. It felt as if he were lying in the middle of a total eclipse of the sun. He looked up and saw something standing over him, blotting out the sunlight with its shadow.

It was huge. Clancy had seen British Columbia totem poles that were shorter than this was. It was hairy, too. It looked as if it lived off a diet of sheep, hair balls, shaggy buffalo, and Highland cattle, so long and furry was its pelt. And it stank worse than a barrel of sun-fouled, maggoty fish.

I am going to die now, Clancy thought. *I am going to get stepped on and eaten and whatever is left of me is most likely going to spill down into this cool running brook to feed the fish.*

Only the Bigfoot did not step on Clancy. It knelt down beside him, poked its arm down into the water, and quicker than you could say the word "catch," that big old Bigfoot had guddled himself up a trout nearly twice as long as Clancy's.

And now it was the Bigfoot's turn to grin.

He knelt there, grinning and gazing at Clancy with the biggest, most beautiful-looking pair of brown eyes Clancy had ever seen.

Clancy couldn't help himself. He laughed out loud, even though another part of him was still certain that the trout would only serve as an appetizer to a Bigfoot-sized pot of stewed Clancy.

The Capstick Bigfoot stood up and blinked, slow like a big old barn cat winking in the sun. Then it turned around and walked into the woodlands, disappearing like eight feet of furry smoke.

The Capstick Bigfoot has not been seen in this area for some time, but there are still a lot of old-timers who believe that it is out there in the thick of the Cape Breton forest. And it's most likely thinking about trout.

The Ghosts of Oak Island

OAK ISLAND

⌒

MAHONE BAY (THE BODY OF WATER, NOT THE TOWN) reaches from New Harbour on the Aspotogan Peninsula in the west to the easternmost point of East Point Island. They say that there is an island in Mahone Bay for every day of the year. These islands come in every shape and size: there's Sheep Island, Rousse Island, Squid Island, Gifford Island, Goat Island, Spectacle Island, Big Tancook Island, Little Tancook Island, Klungemache Island, Crow Island, and many more. Some of the islands are so small that they have never been given names. Some of the islands even disappear with the ebb and the flow of the tide, like ghosts.

But if you are looking to find yourself some stories in these islands, then by far the most legendary of them all has got to be the legend of the mysterious Oak Island Money Pit.

THE BEGINNING

THE STORY BEGINS IN THE 1600S, WHEN LEGEND TELLS US THAT a very old sailor lay on his deathbed and spoke of how he was part of a group of sailors that had helped the dreaded pirate Captain William Kidd bury a horde of treasure on a small island in the gut of Mahone Bay. Oak Island.

"We were told to dig until we reached the gates of hell and then to dig a little deeper," the old sailor explained. "It took us most of the summer. Once we had finished, we sailed away. They took us to another island where they massacred us. Of them all, only I survived."

The story sank away into the depths of legend until 1795, when Daniel McGinnis and his two young friends Anthony Vaughan and Jack Smith paddled out to Oak Island and discovered a strange hollowed depression at the foot of a large oak tree. Younger new-growth oaks sprouted up around the large oak. When the three boys looked a little closer, they were amazed to spot a strangely shaped scar on the belly of the largest overhanging oak limb.

"It looks as if something has been dragged across the bark," Anthony said.

"It reminds me of the grooves the well-rope makes on our old well's windlass," Jack observed. "Yes, sir, something has been roped around this oak limb for certain."

"A horse?" Anthony asked.

"It'd have to be an awfully big horse to cut a groove like that in the bark," Daniel pointed out. "I think something was lowered down right beneath this oak branch—like somebody was digging a well."

"A well or a treasure pit," said Anthony.

"All I see is dirt," Jack said, scratching his head.

"Do you think it's a gold mine?" Anthony asked Daniel. "Buried here underneath this oak tree?"

"Maybe gold," Daniel said. "Maybe a treasure."

"It looks more like a dirt mine to me," Jack pointed out.

So the three of them fetched shovels and a pickaxe and began to dig a hole that would eventually become known as the Oak Island Money Pit. Just less then a metre down into the pit, the diggers unearthed a layer of flagstone, laid out as carefully as if someone had been laying out a courtyard.

"I've never seen stone like this on the island before," Jack said.

"Keep on digging," Daniel ordered.

Three metres down into the Money Pit, the young men came across some oaken planks, old and stained, but laid out just as neatly as a dance floor.

"It has got to be a sign of buried treasure," Daniel said.

The three of them pulled the boards up and were surprised to discover there was nothing underneath but more dirt.

"Keep digging," Anthony said.

None of them needed to be told twice. Treasure fever had taken hold of them hard and fast.

Three metres further found more oak boards. They ripped these up just as quickly.

"There's no treasure here," Anthony said. "No treasure chest either. As far as I can see there is nothing here but more dirt."

"I knew it," Jack said. "We've dug ourselves a dirt mine."

"Keep on digging," Anthony said.

So they kept on digging.

At nine metres they stopped.

"If we dig much farther, we aren't coming back unless we hit China," Daniel said.

So they marked the spot as best they could and covered up their work with a layer of fallen branches.

Six years later, the boys came back to the island. They had been busy over those years—paying for the title to the island, forming a small company, and raising the necessary capital to fund further excavation. This time they were ready.

SIX YEARS LATER

IN 1804, THE BOYS FINALLY RESUMED THEIR DIGGING. EVERY three metres brought them to another layer of oaken planks, followed by a layer of hardened putty and a layer of matted coconut fibre. Just before they reached thirty metres they found a large flat stone, nearly a metre across, with strange hieroglyphic-like engraving upon it. At the thirty-metre mark they found their tenth layer of planks.

"Another seven or eight metres," Jack joked. "And we'll have enough planks to build us a barn to keep all this dirt in."

"This has to be the last layer," Anthony said. "The planks can't go any deeper than this."

Daniel wasn't so certain.

But the boys never found out just how deep the oak planks were laid to, because the next morning when they awoke and lowered themselves down into the pit, they discovered that the pit had been flooded overnight with ten metres of pure salt water.

"I guess that puts us out of the dirt business," Jack said. "We have gone and dug ourselves the world's deepest swimming hole."

Only nobody laughed.

"You get any funnier," Daniel said. "And I may just grab up a pocketful of rocks, jump in, and drown myself."

All the boys could think of doing was to try and dig another hole. They sunk a second shaft directly beside the Money Pit. Just before the thirty-metre level they found what looked to be an impenetrable wooden box, buried in another few metres of mud.

"It has to be the treasure," Jack swore.

"Maybe it is and maybe it isn't," Daniel replied.

They never found out for sure. By the next morning the second tunnel had flooded up as well.

"We're beat," Daniel said.

And beat they were.

The three boys had spent all their collective savings without anything more to show for it but a heap of ancient, weathered oaken boards and half a dozen handfuls of hardened shovel callous.

"Look at the bright side," Anthony said. "Perhaps we can go into business, and advertise ourselves as three well-experienced well-diggers."

Oddly enough, no one laughed.

～

JACK SMITH REFUSES TO QUIT

Over the years Jack Smith continued to buy up pieces of the island, and in 1805 he made another attempt to unearth the Money Pit. Only this time he wasn't digging for himself. Now he was working as a hired hand and consultant for the Onslow Company—a treasure-hunting expedition that had been professionally funded by several Nova Scotia shareholders willing to risk their investment for a chance at recovering a buried treasure.

Jack started by sinking a third shaft about four metres away from the Oak Island Money Pit. When Jack's new crew had reached a depth of thirty-three metres, they dug directly towards the Money Pit, planning to reach the wooden box where they believed the treasure was hidden. But they'd only dug about three more metres downwards before the third tunnel was likewise flooded out.

The years wore on and Jack Smith remained desperately confident that he would find his treasure. In 1849, he formed a third expedition that reopened the original Money Pit and dug even deeper with the aid of a powerful auger drill, such as was used in the mining of Cape Breton coal. The third expedition constructed a platform at the nine-metre mark of the Money Pit and drilled five separate holes, each to a depth of thirty-four metres.

At thirty metres the drill came up against what seemed to be an impenetrable wooden box. The barrier was almost two metres thick and constructed of solid spruce wood. They bored through a layer of clay, another layer of oak planks, and more coconut fibre before eventually coming up with their first real evidence of treasure: three small links from what looked to have been a gold chain or possibly an officer's gold epaulette, followed by fifty-six centimetres of solid metal.

"I knew it," Jack said. "I knew we'd find gold here."

They also discovered a strangely inscribed stone unlike any sort of stone that could be found in the area. In later years, the stone was examined by a Dalhousie University language professor, James Liechti. Professor Liechti used a variation of a very old and very simple substitution code and translated the inscription to read—"FORTY FEET BELOW TWO MILLION POUNDS ARE BURIED."

Then it was discovered that there was a tunnel leading up to the dig site from a hitherto undiscovered man-made beach. It was this tunnel that was responsible for the flooding of all three shafts. Blocking the tunnel with clay and wooden stakes did not help at all, however. The shafts remained flooded with salt water. The water rose and receded with the tide, but it did not recede far enough to make any attempt at diving in and discovering the treasure worthwhile.

There were many further attempts to retrieve the treasure. Fruitless expedition followed fruitless expedition. Fortunes were poured away in a futile attempt to get to the bottom of the mystery of the Money Pit. When one bright treasure hunter thought to fill the Money Pit with red dye, a second flood tunnel was discovered. But plugging the second tunnel did not help either. It was believed that there was a third undiscovered flood tunnel, built as a booby trap by what had to be one of the most fiendish trap-builders of all time to foil would-be fortune hunters, but no one ever found it.

FURTHER SEARCHES

IT WOULD TAKE A LOT MORE ROOM THAN WHAT'S AVAILABLE here to detail each of the numerous expeditions to get to the bottom of the mystery of the Oak Island Money Pit. However, I will do my best to give you a general idea of the scope of the efforts that have been made since those three boys first began digging.

In 1858, the Colchester Company dug up to fifteen pits at the site, using a total of thirty horses to power a set of naval bilge pumps, to no avail. In 1861, that same company brought in a steam engine to aid the pumping. However, the island did not care for the use of such newfangled devices, and a short time after the steam engine was put into action a boiler explosion scalded one of the labourers to death and injured several others. The expedition ground to a halt as men began to talk of the very real possibility that the Oak Island Money Pit might be under some supernatural curse.

In 1865, the newly founded Oak Island Association cleared several more tunnels and found nothing. All that they could determine was that the treasure chamber, perhaps due to the extremely heavy excavation efforts of the treasure hunts, had sunk a little deeper than they thought.

In 1866, the Oak Island Eldorado Company built a coffer dam around the cove in hopes of cutting off the flow of sea water to the Money Pit. This effort also met with failure after an unexpected storm washed the coffer dam away.

In 1897, a second man's life was lost in the treasure hunt when Gold River resident Maynard Kaiser fell twenty-one metres to his death from a bucket hoist when the pulley rope slipped. His fellow workers refused to continue their labour, fearing that the Oak Island curse would kill them all one by one.

I could go on, but suffice it to say, there have been numerous attempts to unearth the mysterious Oak Island Money Pit. From 1890 to 1958, there were a total of fourteen recorded expeditions formed and all of them failed. The area was beginning to look like a piece of Swiss cheese, so many holes and passages had been dug.

The mystery only deepened with each new effort. The expeditions unearthed new layers of iron, coral, coconut fibre, red sand, old oak boards, and mysterious gaps and pockets. The treasure-hunters also found numerous artifacts—more pieces to the puzzle of the Money Pit. They found a scrap of parchment with writing on it, possibly in Latin, along with a quill and black ink. They found a strange stone triangle that may have been part of a seaman's makeshift sextant. They found a pick, an anchor fluke, a miner's seal-oil lamp, and an old axe head.

And in 1965 they found death.

A few years beforehand, Robert Restall, a former circus motorcycle stunt rider, along with his wife and two sons, had acquired the contract to continue explorations on Oak Island. For six years the Restall family had lived there in tents and worked with nothing more than picks and shovels. They'd re-dug the original shaft and uncovered some drainage pipes that flowed from the beach which were responsible for the continuous flooding of the Money Pit. Then, in August 1965, Restall and his oldest son and two other workers were overcome by underground gas. None of them recovered, bringing the island's death toll to six men.

Six men dead and still not a spit of treasure had been unearthed.

Even the three links of gold chain, found in the auger during Jack Smith's earlier 1849 expedition, were suspected of being planted by some worker who was eager to prolong a good-paying job.

THE GHOSTS OF OAK ISLAND

OAK ISLAND REMAINS A TANTALIZING GEOGRAPHICAL ODDITY—A tiny little peanut-shaped oasis at the heart of a treasure hunter's fevered dream. But is it a paranormal oddity as well?

Even before Jack Smith, Anthony Vaughan, and Daniel McGinnis set foot on Oak Island, locals told a tale of how it was guarded by the mysterious glowing spirits of a long-dead pirate crew. It was considered a place of bad luck—a superstition that can certainly be corroborated by the many fortunes that have been squandered there fruitlessly in search of buried treasure, and the lives that have been lost in the process.

Long before the treasure-seekers arrived, the Mi'kmaq believed the island to be a place of bad luck. It was said that any-one who landed on the shore would burst into flame.

Another story states that locals would not go near Oak Island because it was said to be haunted by the ghosts of two fishermen who vanished there in 1720 while investigating strange evening lights.

Many other local folk will tell you of a strange shadowy hound with great sharp teeth and a pair of brightly glowing eyes that lives on the island. This molten-eyed, ebony-hided monster is believed to be the watchdog of Satan himself, keeping a careful blood-stained eye on the treasure.

In 1900, nine-year-old Harris Joudrey—a native of Oak Island—was witness to this eerie hound. He and his friends had been playing a game of hide-and-seek in the nearby woods when he stumbled upon the Money Pit.

"I saw a huge black hound," young Harris reported afterwards. "A hound with a hide as black as the folds on the Devil's cloak. The beast glared at me with blood red eyes that glowed like fiery coals. It growled, low and menacing, in a growl that seemed to emanate from somewhere deep below the earth."

The hound didn't bite Harris.

"It just sat there," Harris went on. "Just growling at me like all it wanted to do was to keep me away from that Money Pit."

Others will tell you they have seen the spirit of an ancient man wearing a bright red frock coat. This spectre will sit upon the roots of the oak tree and wait for the approach of any treasure hunter foolish enough to ask for his advice.

Lastly, there is an old curse that has haunted Oak Island's Money Pit for many years. It has been said that the Oak Island treasure, if it is truly there, will not be found until the last of the oak trees has died and seven treasure hunters have died along with it.

Well, the last of the oak trees perished several years ago, succumbing to a massive infestation of wood ants. To date, six people have perished in the hunt for the secret of the Money Pit. Will a seventh death unlock the mystery?

~

WHAT THE FUTURE HOLDS

Despite a recent change in legislature that ensures that any treasure unearthed on Oak Island or anywhere else in Nova Scotia will become the property of the province, treasure hunters still haven't given up on Oak Island.

The latest plan to unearth the booty involves a scheme to drill a series of holes a metre apart in a ring measuring thirty metres in diameter. The holes will be drilled in such a fashion as to encircle the Money Pit. A pipe header system will then be installed in the holes and brine, chilled to freezing, will be pumped in, creating a perfect ring of frozen soil. The hope is that this frozen ring will seal off the passages that continue to pour water into the Money Pit. The price tag for this latest plan weighs in at about fifteen million dollars.

The Fires of Caledonia Mills

CALEDONIA MILLS

~

ONE OF THE MOST INFAMOUS HAUNTED HOUSES IN NOVA Scotia lies hidden in the heart of Antigonish County, just a short distance from the town of Caledonia Mills. This mystery achieved worldwide fame and has been written up in many different books and newspapers.

A local paranormal investigator was kind enough to give me the exact directions to the location of the farmhouse, but I have chosen not to print those directions here. I do not want to run the risk of being responsible for any ghost hunters who venture out and find themselves lost in the Caledonia Mills woods.

Before you feel cheated, I should tell you that there is no trace of the old farmhouse left, not even evidence of a foundation. There isn't much left around here but memories. If you went to the site all you'd likely find is a handful of dead trees, still standing, and a few boards, beams, and shingles scattered amongst the underbrush. The one thing you would notice, though, is the odd aroma in the air, the lingering scent of ashes and smoke that still hangs over this property.

If you do decide to go, be warned. Don't touch anything you don't have to. Don't take anything home with you or bad luck is sure to follow.

Even though there isn't much left of the farmhouse, folks in Caledonia Mills still remember it and talk about it. And when they talk they tend to whisper.

~

A GAELIC CURSE

WHEN JOHN MACDONALD DIED IN A WESTVILLE COAL-MINING accident, he left behind a wife named Annie and four young children.

"I cannot raise four children by myself," Annie said.

Fortunately, a close friend came to Annie's rescue. Janet MacDonald (no relation) took it upon herself to adopt Mary Ellen, the youngest of the four.

Janet's husband, Alexander, agreed with the decision. "Janet and I are old," Alexander told Annie. "Our house is empty and our children are fully grown. We can give a good, honest home to your daughter. We will be glad if you will allow us to raise her as our own."

Janet and Alexander took Mary Ellen to their home in Caledonia Mills. Their farmhouse wasn't much to look at, just a plain two-storey building with a kitchen out back, and a barn and a few outbuildings scattered about. But it did have one very special feature that wasn't visible to the naked eye: a curse.

It started with an unwanted house guest.

Alexander's younger brother Andrew lived off his lumber camp wages and spent most of his money on gambling and drink. As a result, Andrew fell into the habit of living in his relatives' homes and mooching from their larders.

Alexander and his brothers and sisters had long ago learned to indulge Andrew in his habit, but Janet wasn't nearly as patient with the scoundrel. She got tired of coming home to find him drunk in the kitchen.

One cold and stormy November evening in 1903, Janet had Alexander throw his brother out of their house. "I will put up with his drinking no longer," she told her husband. "Either he goes or I do."

It did not take Alexander long to come to his decision. The truth was, he had grown tired of his brother's wastrel ways and was secretly all too happy to turn the moocher out into the night.

But Andrew was determined to have the last word. Before he stepped out into the cold, unwelcome night air, he turned to his brother and his wife and said, "You both will be driven out from your house on a worse night than this one." He spoke these words in Gaelic so that the spirits would hear them and heed them.

And then he walked away.

～

THE MAD WOMAN

IN ADDITION TO THE SPECTRE OF ANDREW'S CURSE, THE MacDonalds of Caledonia Mills lived beneath the shadow of Janet's mother, who in her late eighties had fallen prey to dementia. Alexander had quietly arranged to have his mother-in-law committed to the County Home, but Janet would not have it. She, just as quietly, had arranged for her mother to leave the County Home and move in with them.

The old woman was kept locked in her bedroom for her own safety. But locked door or not, she was often found wandering about the house screaming. On April 27, 1900, a house guest was witness to one of these late night seizures. The old woman was raving like a banshee when Janet burst into her bedroom and shrieked out, "I hope the Devil in hell comes and takes you before nine o'clock tomorrow morning!"

It was at this moment that the house guest swore he saw an eerie sight. "A small black dog padded in through the house and walked directly into the old woman's bedroom and barked three times before disappearing under the bed," the guest testified. "The bedroom was searched afterwards, but there was no trace of a dog to be found."

The following morning, Janet's mother was found dead in her bedroom.

These are the shadows that young Mary Ellen grew up beneath. Things would grow darker still.

POLTERGEIST PRANKS

A "POLTERGEIST" IS USUALLY DESCRIBED AS A NASTY HOUSE-hold spirit who takes delight in flinging furniture, utensils, and other personal belongings about. The word stems from Germanic roots and translates generally to "noisy spirit." Poltergeists have been reported in nations and cultures across the world, and they often seem to manifest when one or more of the occupants of the house are in their teenage years.

The haunting activities in Caledonia Mills began on a very simple and playful note. Kitchen mats were found rolled up and leaned against the line of fence that divided the MacDonald property from its neighbours'. Then pots and pans and other kitchen implements started showing up beside the fence.

Then the animals began to stray. Alexander would often find his horse and cattle wandering in the yard after he had corralled them or locked them in the barn. So Alexander started getting more creative in his methods of restraint, tying knot upon knot in an effort to put an end to the mysterious incidents. But every morning he would wake up to find the livestock roaming where they shouldn't have been.

"Perhaps it's the horse," Janet suggested. "He is awfully smart for a dapple pony."

So Alexander traded his horse for another. But still the untying continued. After a time Alexander came to expect it as he expected the rising of the sun. Every night he would secure the horse and cows in the barn, only to wake to find them wandering through the back field. Some mornings he would even find the horse's mane and tail braided.

"It's the Lutin," Janet swore, blaming it on the Highland faerie-folk, who were known for such trickery. "They have always been fascinated with knots and hitches of all sorts. And they certainly love braiding a horse's mane."

Whatever the reason was, the strange untying of knots and the release of the MacDonald livestock continued until the winter of 1922, when the mysterious fires first began.

~

THE FIRST FIRE

THE FIRST FIRE TOOK PLACE ON SATURDAY, JANUARY 7, 1922. Alexander was up early to light the kitchen stove when he noticed that the wall and ceiling were charred.

"That won't do," he said. "The pipes must need cleaning." He took the pipe down and made certain it was clear of soot. Then he reassembled it and made equally certain that it was far enough away from the wall and ceiling to ensure no further damage.

He was even careful to make sure that the fire was out by four o'clock that afternoon. It wouldn't do to let the farm burn down.

That evening Janet smelled smoke. When Alexander investigated, he discovered an upholstered chair and lounge were both smouldering. Oddly enough, both pieces of furniture were some distance away from the stove. He hastily extinguished the fires and sat up worrying and fretting for most of the night.

The next day brought five more fires burning in the loft above the kitchen. That evening, before retiring, seventy-year-old Alexander clambered up onto the roof and poured a bucket of water down the chimney to make certain that the fire was completely extinguished.

An hour later Alexander and Janet awoke to the smell of smoke. They found several more fires burning in the kitchen loft. Throughout the rest of the evening Alexander kept a fitful watch as fire after fire broke out.

The next day was quiet. Alexander took advantage of the momentary lull and removed the floorboards in the kitchen loft. He swept and cleaned them, making certain they were clear of any debris that might somehow catch fire.

The next day, the fires resumed. Janet and Alexander watched in surprised terror as a fire spontaneously ignited above their heads, again in the kitchen loft. Janet clambered up the ladder to the loft, tore the smouldering board from the floor, and flung it out the window into the snow below.

A half hour later, the fires continued. A wall over the door leading from the kitchen into the main section of the house caught fire. Several other fires broke out in the main house. Alexander, fearful for his family, sent Janet and Mary Ellen out on that stormy evening to go and get whatever help they could find. They bundled up in parkas and galoshes and made their way to their nearest neighbours, the MacGillivrays, who lived two kilometres up the road from them.

Dan and Leo MacGillivray and their visiting brother-in-law, Duncan MacDonald, accompanied the two women back to help Alexander fight the flames. When they arrived everything seemed normal. The four men went over the house with a fine-toothed comb, looking for any trace of fire, but could find none.

Finally, Dan MacGillivray went home. Everything seemed fine to him. Leo and Duncan stayed where they were, however. It just didn't seem right to them to abandon a neighbour who had asked for their help.

Their caution proved wise. A short time after Dan left, another fire broke out. This time it was on a parlour window blind. A half hour later, a calendar hanging by the parlour stove caught fire. The parlour stove wasn't lit at the time. In fact, it hadn't been lit in several days. A few minutes later, a bed in the guest room caught fire. The dog's bed also caught fire. For the next couple of hours, the MacDonalds and their neighbours were kept busy patrolling the house for fires and extinguishing them.

In all, thirty-eight fires broke out over the run of that evening. The Fire-Spook kept Alexander, Janet, Leo, Duncan, and Mary Ellen very busy with blazes that broke out in locked dresser drawers and closed kitchen cupboards. By morning there were at least five centimetres of water pooled up on the dining room floor. But even that did not help. A wet dish rag, sopping in a puddle, spontaneously ignited and burned to nothing but blackened ash. The stink from that fire was phenomenally oppressive.

Leo MacGillivray had this to say about the event: "We were in the house about half an hour when the whole house seemed to be strangely illuminated, just as sudden and bright as if a short circuit had occurred on a high-tension wire. The blaze seemed brighter in the parlour so I made a dash for that room. The window blind was enveloped in flames. I tore it off the window and managed to save about half of it. The flame was a pale blue and the only thing that I could liken it to was a short circuit. The flame was not hot and it did not even singe the hair on the back of my hands or eyebrows."

"I saw paper burning when it was wet," Duncan MacGillivray testified afterwards. "There was no gasoline or anything inflammable around the house."

At one point during the night, Duncan MacDonald was sent home to call for help because the MacDonalds' telephone line wasn't working in the intensity of the local storm. He made it to the MacGillivrays' and called the authorities, but most of them were busy fighting the effects of the storm, and they couldn't make it out there until morning.

Mike MacGillivray and John F. Kenny were the first people to arrive at the farmhouse the next morning. "We saw a small black dog, the colour of soot, trailing behind us," Kenny later stated. "It followed us to the farmhouse and then disappeared. I imagine it ran off into the woods."

When MacGillivray and Kenny got there, the first thing they saw was a bare arm waving a white rag from the upstairs window.

"Are they surrendering?" Kenny asked.

"Let's go see," MacGillivray said.

When they walked into the kitchen and asked about the arm waving from the upstairs window, Leo MacGillivray assured them that no one had left the kitchen.

"It must have been a ghost then," Kenny joked.

No one laughed.

"We aren't staying here another night," Alexander decided. "If these fires keep up, we are going to wake up burned to death in our beds." So the McDonalds packed their belongings and spent their first night away from home at the MacGillivray residence.

The following morning, they moved into a house in town that was owned and rented by Duncan MacDonald. Secretly, the MacGillivrays were more than happy to see the flame-cursed family out from beneath their roof.

~

WORD GETS OUT

NEWS OF THE EVENTS SPREAD. W. H. DENNIS, THE EDITOR OF THE *Halifax Herald* and *Evening Mail*, picked up the story and dispatched a *Herald* reporter by the name of Harold Whidden to the scene of the events.

"Get me the facts on this," Dennis told Whidden.

Whidden and a photographer spoke to the witnesses and took photos of the house. Whidden took down their stories in great detail and was a little disappointed that no further blazes broke out while he was on the premises. He was equally disappointed that there seemed to be no explanation for these mysterious fires.

But that didn't stop W. H. Dennis. "We'll hold a contest," he said to Whidden. "We'll offer a reward to the reader who sends in the most plausible explanation."

The answers that were mailed in were plentiful and varied. Some said it was the work of spirits. Others suggested radio waves or the presence of some sort of mysterious acid or mineral beneath the property. Others suggested a slow-burning chemical compound applied previously by some unknown enemy of the family. And one person was even convinced that the fires were caused by a firefly infestation. In all there were over 150 theories sent in to the *Herald*.

In the end they decided that the theories presented still weren't enough. So they sent for an expert.

～

CALL FOR A DETECTIVE

IN FEBRUARY 1922, A FORMER PICTOU POLICE CHIEF NAMED Peter Owen Carroll, known as "Peachie" to his friends, declared his interest in the Caledonia Mills case. Peachie was at that time an official provincial detective.

"I will go to Caledonia Mills and live in the house in question," Peachie declared. "I won't leave until I've got to the bottom of this."

Harold Whidden agreed to accompany Peachie to the Caledonia Mills farmhouse. By this time the farmhouse had been emptied of furniture and belongings, but that didn't stop the fearless investigators. The two men set up a portable stove in the dining room and heaped fresh hay on the floor for mattresses. But a winter storm blew up and the wind howled through the old farmhouse and the little portable stove they had brought for heat proved sadly inadequate.

"I can't think of a more perfect place to catch my death of pneumonia," Whidden complained.

Later that evening the storm abated and Alexander MacDonald made his way along the wintered-over road, walking almost two kilometres to bring the two investigators a home-cooked meal. "It seemed the least I could do for two fellows who were so willing to risk their lives to get to the bottom of this situation," he later said.

At midnight the trouble began. It started with a banging outside, as if someone were pounding on the front door and trying to get in. Only there was no one at the door. Then they heard footsteps creaking across the floorboards. Then Peachie was slapped, as if by an invisible palm. The noises continued throughout the long cold night.

The next morning, Whidden decided to call it quits. The weather was too much for him. Peachie stayed on for a few more weeks and over that time he continued to question all the witnesses of the fire. Although he hadn't actually witnessed any spontaneous fires himself, Peachie had this to say about the Caledonia Mills farmhouse: "I firmly believe that neither the fires nor the strange occurrences were the work of human hands. In my opinion, no one could have any conception of the case without first visiting the house and going into every crumb of evidence with the utmost care."

However, the authorities were still unconvinced.

In March 1922, the *Herald* invited a psychic researcher, Walter F. Prince of New York, to come to Caledonia Mills and to further investigate the mysterious fires. After a week of interviews and some time spent looking over the flame-scarred farmhouse, Prince came to the conclusion that the fires and banging and mysterious loosing of livestock were all the work of young Mary Ellen.

"The girl has the mind of a six-year-old child," Prince declared. "She is obsessed with the spiritual world and has demonstrated all of the symptoms of someone who is suffering from delusions inspired by childhood trauma. In my opinion the fires were set by human hand, devoid of guilt."

But Peachie Carroll disagreed strongly, stating, "Mary Ellen is as bright and alert as any sixteen-year-old girl brought up by her grandparents. There is no definite or satisfactory evidence that any fires broke out without Mary Ellen being close at hand to her grandparents."

Peachie further argued that Alexander and the other men had spent a long night fighting fires that could not have been set by such a young girl. He then went on to issue a public challenge of Prince's findings, saying that the researcher was a fraud and a liar.

∼

QUIET ENDINGS

THE NEXT TWO MONTHS WERE FAIRLY UNEVENTFUL. IN EARLY May 1922, the MacDonalds returned to the farmhouse and put in their crops. And on May 18, 1922, the fires began again. The MacDonalds put up with the fires until June, keeping very quiet for fear of further publicity. Then they left the farm and the Caledonia Mills area and moved to Alder River, where they moved in with their daughter, Mrs. William Quirk.

One year later, Alexander MacDonald died of influenza, at the age of seventy-six. Janet MacDonald followed her husband seven years later.

Mary Ellen's trail is a little harder to unravel. She lived in Alder River for a short while and then moved to Antigonish and worked as a domestic servant for the Bonner family on St. Ninian

Street. She left the Bonners' service shortly after a distant relative from New Glasgow came to her with a scheme for fame and fast money, claiming that she could make a fortune being displayed on the stage as a sort of theatrical freak show. After a few weeks of dusting and sweeping, this life sounded very tempting to Mary Ellen, so she left for New Glasgow.

But when Mary Ellen arrived in New Glasgow, her relative quickly learned that she was more interested in kindling a series of tawdry backdoor romances than participating in a freak show. One of these romances soon took hold and Mary Ellen left New Glasgow, accompanied by a Mr. Jackson. The pair travelled to Montreal and Mary Ellen found life in the big city to be intoxicating.

Unfortunately, when she arrived in Montreal, the only form of employment Mary Ellen could find was that of a waitress. Mary Ellen didn't take very readily to being a waitress. Her feet hurt, her back hurt, and her pockets were mostly empty.

She soon left Mr. Jackson to his own devices and ran off to the nickel town of Sudbury, Ontario, certain that she would strike up some sort of a relationship with a well-to-do miner. She soon found herself married to a man named Austin "Red" McGuire. She and Austin opened up a rooming house for miners, where Austin bootlegged cheap illicit whiskey and Mary Ellen peddled something just as cheap and illicit. The rooming house quickly developed quite a reputation and became known locally as "The Bucket of Blood."

Mary Ellen died in the early summer of 1988, several years after Austin passed away. She was eighty years old. Her funeral was a quiet ceremony attended by a few friends and acquaintances.

There were no further reports of phantom fires after the MacDonalds left Caledonia Mills, but people still keep a path beaten to the spot where the farmhouse once stood.

The Tale of the Screeching Bridge

PARRSBORO

~

I LOOKED DEEPLY INTO THE STORY OF THE SCREECHING Bridge while I was researching this book, and as so often happens when dealing with folklore and recollection, I came across three different versions of this story. It seems that most storytellers could not determine just where in Parrsboro the Screeching Bridge lay.

So I spoke to a Parrsboro historian and storyteller named Conrad Byers, who gave me the exact location of the bridge. I'll tip my hat to Conrad for filling me in on the facts behind this folklore.

AS THE MILL WHEEL TURNS

IN 1800, JOSIAH DAVISON AND HIS FAMILY BUILT A TIDAL DAM gristmill across the Parrsboro River. When they were building the mill, they also incorporated a bridge alongside the dam to encourage traffic and trade. There had always been a crossing at this particular point in the river, due to a natural outcrop of base rock, but up until this point travellers had been obliged to wade across the river and the attached tidal marsh either on foot or on horseback.

Josiah became very popular after building his bridge, which certainly didn't hurt business. Some people thought the bridge was such a great idea that they began building their own mills in the area. The spot quickly became known as Mill Village, and the stretch of water became known as the Mill Creek. Understandably enough, Josiah's bridge was known as the Mill Creek Bridge.

And it was here on the Mill Creek Bridge, on a Halloween night in the mid-nineteenth century, that terror struck.

HALLOWEEN HEARTBREAK

OCTOBER 31 IS WHAT THE OLD PEOPLE CALL "THE NIGHT OF THE long moon," since it's one of the longest nights of the year. Some Christians will tell you that on the last night in October, which they call All Hallow's Night, the walls between the worlds wear thin. According to these sources, this is the one night of the year that Satan himself is given his freedom and allowed to walk the night free and unhampered, spreading mischief and harm wherever he cares to.

Each year on the evening of October 31, the old Druids would sing to the oak trees and the Celts would go from door to door gathering offerings of food and kindling. They did this in order to raise up sacred bonfires to light the way to the far country for the spirits of those who had died throughout the year. At the end of the evening they would carry the embers from the bonfire in a hollowed-out gourd, turnip, or pumpkin to relight each family's hearth fire and bring good luck for all in the coming new year. Huge steaming dishes of cabbage and potato and turnip and all manner of root crops harvested late in the fall would be boiled up and a great feast would be given so people from far and wide could warm their insides against the cold to come. It was a time of getting ready and grinning against winter.

However, on this particular All Hallow's Eve (or Halloween as we call it nowadays), Marie MacDonald walked in sorrow. She had not felt like celebrating since young Rory had decided that he no longer loved her.

Marie had done everything she could think of to rekindle Rory's love for her. She had eaten salt fish in hopes that Rory would come to her in a dream and bring her a cool glass of water. Only Rory hadn't come. She had peeled an apple and threw the peeling over her shoulder in hopes that it would spell out Rory's name. Only whatever the peeling spelled out must have been written in some other language, because Marie certainly couldn't read it.

So now, while other people were out gathering the rotten cabbages from the fields and gardens and chucking them at doorways for the fun of it, Marie walked the night alone in silence. Marie felt she had more in common with the rotten cabbages than she did with anything remotely resembling fun.

"You ought to take your hand mirror out to the river and walk backwards along the shore," her best friend, Meg, told her. "You will certainly see your true love in its reflection." Marie wasn't certain if the mirror plan was going to work any better than the apple peeling or the salt fish had, but by this point she was willing to try anything.

"It'll be Rory," Marie told Meg. "That's the only boy for me. No one else will show up in that mirror."

"I don't know if Tammy Whitaker would agree with you," Meg said. "I saw her walking arm in arm with Rory over the Mill Creek Bridge."

Marie didn't listen.

CAUGHT IN GLASS

As far as Marie could tell, the wind was blowing from the coldest corner of the world right directly down the Mill Creek. She knew it was too cold to be out that night, but she was determined to try that mirror trick.

"I'll catch his heart in the glass of the mirror," she told herself. "There is no other boy for me."

Only she had been walking back and forth alongside the water for so long that she had worn a trough in the dirt clear up to her ankles.

"The only thing I'm getting from this river-walking is muddy feet," Marie said. "I must be doing something wrong."

The old mill wheel turned in the current in front of her. Marie stopped and watched it turn for a while. Then she turned her gaze to the bridge.

"I bet he'd be walking up there," Marie decided. "There's nothing more romantic than walking across a lonely bridge."

So she walked on over to the end of the bridge. She crossed it once. She didn't see anything but the wind in the front of her face and it blew so cold that tears came to her eyes.

"I need to walk backwards," Marie said. "That's how Meg told me to and it makes sense when you think of it. What else is love but blind faith, walking backwards on a bridge on the coldest night of the year?"

Marie held the hand mirror up directly in front of her face and walked backwards against the wind. She had to admit that she felt a lot more comfortable this way even though it made her scared and nervous walking backwards like she was, which only goes to show you that there are a great many ways that love will lead a person to do an awful lot of stupid things.

"Never mind," she told herself. "If this will get me Rory than I will gladly walk backwards to the ends of the earth."

Which was right about when she saw something in the mirror. *It's Rory!* she thought to herself. Only it wasn't Rory.

It was the Devil himself, out for a midnight stroll on the one night of the year that the powers above allowed him free reign on this earth. And here was a chance to make mischief with nothing more than a grin.

"Boo," that old Devil said.

The Devil grinned so hard that the mirror cracked in two. His eyes blazed in the mirror's reflection like a candle in the heart of a jack-o'-lantern.

Marie screamed, jumped up, and ran straight off the bridge. She screamed all the way down to the frigid water and as the tide caught hold of her and dragged her down to the open sea. And that old Devil laughed and laughed the whole time.

~

THE STORY TODAY

FOR MANY DAYS THE TOWNSFOLK SEARCHED UP AND DOWN THE water for Marie, but to no avail. There was no trace of her. They decided amongst themselves that Marie had very likely taken her own life, preferring to jump into the embrace of death rather than to continue on with a broken heart.

Rory thought that was pretty funny and he laughed about it often—until Tammy grew disgusted with his cold heart and slapped him in the face.

Every Halloween night for many years after the cursed evening of Marie's disappearance, her screams could be heard piercing the air around the Mill Creek Bridge. And so, for a long time after her death, this area was known as "Screecher's Hollow."

But over the years the tide of time worked its gentle erasing magic. The mills closed down. Mill Village became nothing more than a sleepy dead-end road with a half a dozen houses scattered down it.

"Nothing down there but frogs croaking," the locals would say.

And there were a lot of frogs, which is why the sleepy little village became known as Frog Hollow, and the bridge that spanned the river became known as the Frog Hollow Bridge.

In the late nineteenth century, Frog Hollow experienced a boom in population. Some people felt that the name "Frog Hollow" was too rustic for what they hoped was going to become a populated area, and so, on October 18, 1890—just one year after the town of Parrsboro was first incorporated—the village's name was changed to Lower Victoria Street.

Most of the older folk know better than that and still refer to the area as Frog Hollow. The original Mill Creek Bridge, which is now known as Whitehall Bridge, stands to this day, and some folks say that on cold Halloween nights you can still hear the sound of Marie's screams.

Three Selkies for Three Brothers

CAPE BRETON

HERE IS ACTUALLY AN AREA KNOWN AS CAPE BRETON situated upon Cape Breton Island. It is located on the easternmost corner of the island, a little jut of granite about ten kilometres east of the Fortress of Louisbourg and west of Scaterie Island. Originally named Cap Breton, it is known for its high-breaking waves, rocky eroded shores, and steep sea cliffs. It is a hard land for hard men and even harder women.

Local storytellers tell a tale of three brothers—Donald, Clancy, and Rook—from the area who swore a sacred oath at their dying mother's bedside that they would all get out of trouble and become honest married men before another summer had come and passed.

"Well, where shall we find these wives?" asked Donald one evening soon afterward. Donald was the youngest brother and he had hair the colour of dead straw. "It's not as if they are growing wild on the Cape Breton beach."

There were some who said that poor young Donald had about as much common sense as a heap of mouldy summer hay, but most who knew him were kinder to the lad and just called him simple.

"Billy Regan has himself a fine bride," Clancy said. "I bet I could steal her from him, if I put my mind to it."

Clancy was the oldest brother. He had hair as red as a burning radish. Clancy was good with his fists and some say he had a temper as well.

"We don't need to steal them, and we won't have to work too hard to find them," Rook said. "For I know of a spot where the women do grow wild on the beach."

Rook was the middle child. Living in the middle had taught him how to use his wits. Rook's hair was as black as a crow's midnight shadow and some said he had the eyes of a thief.

"So what is your plan, brother?" Clancy asked.

"We'll go down to the water tonight when the moon is fat and full and the selkies come up to dance," Rook replied.

Now, as every good Cape Bretoner knows, a selkie is a being that lives in the water in the shape of a seal, but peels off its sealskin and comes ashore as a human on full moon nights. Then the selkies frolic and dance with one another until the night has burned down into morning.

"And we'll steal their sealskins and hide them," Rook continued as the three of them approached the rocky shore. "Then those selkie girls will do whatever we ask them to."

"But what if we don't love them?" Donald asked.

Clancy cracked Donald hard enough on the back of his skull to knock a few freckles loose from his cheekbones. "They'll do whatever we tell them to do," Clancy said. "What more does a man want of a woman?"

As the three boys clambered onto the shore, the moon looked down and winked just once as a cloud passed before it. When the cloud had finished passing, the boys looked out to see the water filled with selkies.

The three brothers held their breath and stared as the selkies rose up out of the water and shed their sealskins.

And who could blame them? There is no other beauty as true and as pure as the beauty of the selkie.

"I'll steal the first one," Clancy said. "For I'm a better thief than either of you."

And saying that, Clancy crept and scuttled and stole along the rock and through the shadow until he found a selkie sealskin neatly folded in a cradle of kelp-draped driftwood.

"I'll steal the second," Rook said. "For it was my idea in the first place."

And Rook stole up and found himself a sealskin that he believed to be even finer than his brother Clancy had found.

"I guess that leaves me," Donald said.

And he walked down and picked up the first sealskin he came to.

When the moon sank down beneath the waves and the sunrise embered up from the distant hills, the selkies slid into their sealskins and slipped away into the early morning water—all but three of them, that is, which was how the three brothers found themselves their three selkie brides.

Mind you, it wasn't as easy as it sounds. The selkies were unhappy on the land, but because the brothers had their sealskins hidden away they had no choice but to learn to accept their new lives.

Once every month, when the moon rose high in the evening sky, the three selkie women would walk down to the rocks and watch their sisters dancing amidst the waves. They did not dare to approach any closer for they knew that if any of the selkies saw them they would tear them to pieces for the shame of losing their sealskins. Still, they had to come and watch.

The years passed by and each selkie woman gave her husband three fine children. One fateful morning, Rook bragged to his oldest son about where he had hidden his wife's sealskin. The son, who was of course part selkie, immediately ran to his mother and informed her. "Your skin is hidden under a rock in the barn, beneath a bale of hay."

And that night the selkie stole out to the barn and rolled the bale of hay away and turned the rock over and found her sealskin. As quick as you can say "flit," the selkie pulled on her sealskin and returned to the water, abandoning her husband and her home and her children—even the son who had told her where her skin was hidden.

"More fool you," Clancy laughed at his brother the next morning. "A man should keep his mouth closed around his children and his woman."

The next night, Donald's selkie bride came to him in tears.

"I miss the sea," she told him. "And I miss dancing in the waves with my selkie sisters. Won't you give me the skin for just one night? I promise to return when the full moon has passed and serve you as your wife."

"How do I know you won't run away?" Donald asked.

"I only want to dance with the waves just one more time," the selkie said. "Or else I may die."

And Donald, being a soft-hearted man, handed the sealskin to his bride and watched as she walked back into the water and turned into a seal. Tears rolled down his cheeks because he knew, deep in his heart, that she would never return.

"More fool you," Clancy laughed at Donald the next morning, even louder than he had laughed at Rook. "A man should share nothing that he cannot afford to lose."

But the thought of how his brothers had both lost their selkie wives worried Clancy to death. So that night he built a great fire. Then he unlocked the trunk that he kept his selkie wife's sealskin in, pulled the skin out, and threw it into the flames, believing that if he burned it to ashes his wife would never be able to return to the sea. But as soon as the sealskin hit the flames, the oil in the skin ignited in a blazing inferno. The fire rose up so quickly and menacingly that Clancy couldn't control it. The fire devoured

Clancy's house and Clancy's children and then Clancy himself died screaming in the flames.

The next morning, Donald's selkie bride walked up out of the water and back home to him. She had decided to come back to the land because she missed the man who had given her the freedom to dance.

As for Rook, he lived alone the rest of his days. Not even his children, who blamed him for the loss of their mother, would speak to him anymore. He spent long, lonely years staring at the waves of the cold Atlantic shoreline, wondering just how in the world his younger and ever-so-stupider brother had turned out to be so much smarter than him.

Ivy Clings to this Lodge

WHITE POINT

~

THE WHITE POINT RESORT LODGE IS A WELL-KNOWN centre of hospitality and comfort, located about one hundred and fifty kilometres southwest of Halifax on Highway 103. White Point Lodge first got into business back in 1928 as a private fishing and hunting lodge. At that time, the resort consisted of a few scattered cabins on the beach, a dining room, and an eight-room main lodge built in a traditional rustic manner.

In 1931, the lodge added its very first tennis court. A golf course was set up shortly afterward. Since then, the lodge has blossomed into a popular year-round, 160-bedroom resort.

The lodge has a history of ghost sightings, with three distinct ghosts making occasional appearances. Each has its own story and truly unique personality.

~

IVY'S ROOTS

HOWARD ELLIOT HAD ENJOYED A LONG HISTORY IN THE HOS-pitality business. He'd spent years running both the Sword and

Anchor in Chester and the Dresden Arms in Halifax. In 1928, he helped found the White Point Resort Lodge. Accompanying Howard in this endeavour was his lovely wife, Ivy.

Ivy immediately set to work managing the resort's food and beverage department. She proved herself to be an extremely difficult boss to work for, maintaining the strictest of standards for dining room staff. Ivy was tough and uncompromising. If a piece of cutlery was set in the wrong place, she would spot it and would very certainly bring it to the offending waiter's attention. She had a bad temper and would often throw kitchen utensils when she was angry—being the founder's wife meant that you could get away with that sort of behaviour.

No one remembers just exactly how or when Ivy finally died, but it was likely after her losing her temper just one too many times. And apparently even in death Ivy hasn't been able to find peace. It is said that to this day she still haunts the lodge, throwing temper tantrums just like she did when she was alive.

~

THE THREE GHOSTS

MOST OF THE EMPLOYEES AT WHITE POINT HAVE ENCOUNTERED Ivy's ghost in one way or another. Some of them have heard footsteps coming from the front of the dining room towards the kitchen. Some have watched as doors swung open suddenly or slammed shut, lights have turned on and off at unexpected moments, and spoons and ladles have jumped off their s-hooks and clattered noisily to the kitchen floor.

Others have reported actually seeing Ivy. Hotel employees have seen her walking across the floor in a long, flowing white pantsuit. Groundskeepers have seen her walking through snow or along the rocks of the beach. Ivy is notoriously shy and is usually only spotted in the deep winter, and almost never appears before hotel guests.

Ivy's isn't the only ghost haunting the grounds of the White Point Resort. There have also been reports of a ghostly caretaker roaming the area. "Many people believe the ghost of an older gentleman named Danny roams White Point," Bruce Clattenburg, who has been the night engineer at White Point Lodge for the last ten years, reports. "Danny was the caretaker here in the wintertime and the chef in the summer. He stayed in Cabin 20. Today it is unit 137. I worked with him between 1978 and 1979 and he was a great guy and a really good friend."

According to Bruce, Danny and Ivy were close friends. After Ivy died, Danny would often be spotted having long conversations with thin air. Sometimes he was seen sitting in his cabin or at a picnic table sharing a drink and a conversation with someone who could not be seen. Danny swore that it was Ivy. He maintained that she came back at every opportunity and spent time with him.

There is also a third ghost at White Point Lodge, the spirit of a young boy whose family lived in the area in the 1920s. The boy reportedly drowned while rafting off White Point, although his body was never found. He was nine years old at the time.

The boy's ghost is seen rarely, but he is always described as wearing old-style overalls and a white shirt. He is usually spotted on the rocks of the beach or occasionally out on a raft or a boat.

~

SID'S STORY

ONE OF THE BEST STORIES I'VE EVER HEARD ABOUT IVY WAS told to me by a bartender named Sid, who was working as a waiter at the time of the sighting.

On the night in question, Sid was working late to get ready for a large convention banquet being held the next day.

"I was tired," Sid told me. "And I misplaced a dessert spoon on the table arrangement. By the time I had realized my mistake

I was nearly done setting the entire dining room and would have to go back and reset each of the tables."

Sid shook his head ruefully.

"At that point the lights shut off. It took me a good five minutes to find my way to the proper switch and turn them on again. When the lights came back on I was surprised to see a dessert spoon flying at me. It clanged off my forehead and nearly rose up a goose egg. I picked the spoon up and looked again and was amazed to see that all of the misplaced cutlery had been corrected for me."

He grinned at this point and threw me a wink.

"I don't really know if there is such a thing as ghosts," Sid said. "But I do believe that Ivy was looking out for me that night. She reset the tables properly and then flung that spoon just to remind me not to make the same mistake twice."

Mrs. Murray's Five Crying Babies

NEW GLASGOW

~

IT WAS A COLD AND BITTER DAY ON WEDNESDAY, FEBRUARY 18, 1880, when Dr. William Fraser and a pharmacist by the name of James Jackson hitched up a wagon and clambered aboard to make the rough and dangerous seven-kilometre journey from New Glasgow to a tiny Nova Scotia settlement that was known back then as Little Egypt. The snow was blowing straight at the men as they drove, which made it awfully hard to see.

"Horses, you keep your eyes open," the doctor warned his team. "Or we're most likely apt to pass right by the homestead and keep on riding right into the open mouth of Little Harbour."

The horses must have been listening closely because they eventually found their way to the doorstep of sixty-five-year-old Adam Murray and his thirty-seven-year-old wife, Marie. According to Dr. Fraser, Marie Murray was a strong and healthy woman who was already the mother of seven children, and was about to give birth to five more—at the same time. Unbeknownst to her, Marie Murray was expecting quintuplets.

Within an hour, all five children were delivered. There were three girls and two boys, each as tiny and petite as a little china doll.

The news of the births spread throughout the area within hours. Local folk were soon knocking politely at the Murrays' door, dropping by to see the babies first-hand and to offer up small gifts of food and money to help the family with their unexpected burden.

Marie named the babies after the doctor and the pharmacist, two other prominent members of the community, and the children's own grandmother. Elizabeth MacGregor Murray, the largest baby, was sixteen inches long and weighed in at three pounds, fourteen ounces. Margaret MacQueen Murray was fifteen and a quarter inches long and weighed a strapping three pounds, six ounces. William Fraser Murray reached fourteen and a quarter inches and weighed three pounds, four ounces. James Jackson Murray was fifteen and five-eighths inches long and weighed three pounds exactly. Finally, the smallest of the lot, little Jeanette Rankin Murray reached a length of thirteen and a half inches and weighed in at two pounds, eight ounces.

Sadly, because the babies were so small, their chances of reaching maturity were fairly slim. Three died before the first evening had passed. A fourth died the following morning. And the fifth, little Elizabeth MacGregor, lasted three days before closing her eyes and breathing out the strains of her final lullaby.

An hour before Elizabeth passed away, a newspaper reporter showed up at the Murray residence and persuaded her grieving parents to allow him to line up the five babies—the four dead and the one living—for a photograph that would appear in newspapers across Canada. The publication of this photo raised quite a commotion for the Murrays. This was the first birth of quintuplets recorded in Canada—over half a century before the famous

Dionne quintuplets were born in 1934 in Corbeil, Ontario—and the news soon grabbed the attention of people across the country.

Shortly after the photo was published, the Murrays received an offer from famed circus showman P. T. Barnum, who wanted to buy the five tiny bodies—which the Murrays couldn't bury until the spring thaw came—and have them mummified for display in his circus. The Murrays refused Barnum's offer flatly. When he continued to pressure them, they buried the children in their basement, fearing that a public burial site might be pilfered by unscrupulous grave robbers.

Soon afterward, a local New Glasgow businessman, who preferred to keep his identity strictly anonymous, came forward and offered to bury the infants in an unmarked portion of his family plot in New Glasgow's Riverside Cemetery so that they could lie in sanctified ground. The Murrays gladly accepted the man's offer, and the five babies were finally laid to rest in a proper grave.

But to this day, local residents swear that on certain nights you can hear the gentle haunting sound of five tiny infants wailing for their mother from the heart of New Glasgow's Riverside Cemetery.

The Sad Story of the Stormy Petrel

MAITLAND

~

THE STORMY PETREL WAS LONG CONSIDERED TO BE A HARbinger of bad weather and worse luck.

Maritimers often refer to this little grey bird as the "Devil Bird" or "Mother Carey's Chicken."

Stormy petrels are seen year-round from Nova Scotia and Newfoundland to South America and even as far east as the African coast. Flocks of these dark, swift-flying birds will shoot down out of the clouds and wing past a ship to land in its wake, hoping to catch whatever scraps fall from behind the stern of the vessel.

Some would say that naming a ship after these bad luck birds is a sure way to invite the worst kind of misfortune. Captain David Douglas would likely agree.

A LUMBER RUN

ONE FINE DAY IN 1890, THE LUMBER BARQUE *STORMY PETREL*, heavily laden with a cargo of freshly felled timber, unfurled its worn and battered canvas to the cruel Bay of Fundy winds as its captain, David Douglas of Maitland, steered it patiently into the open Atlantic. Captain Douglas was bound for the Bordeaux coastline in far-off France.

The weather was kind to Douglas over the first part of his journey. He was heartily glad of this, for he had his wife, his three-year-old-daughter, and his five-year-old son on board.

Little Eddie Douglas, the captain's son, got along well with the crew of the *Stormy Petrel*, playing games of hide-and-go-seek and tag with them whenever he could. One day, as they were midway across the Atlantic, Eddie splashed water at a crewman and went running from him, giggling. The laughing sailor chased him in good-natured pursuit. Unfortunately, as Eddie was fleeing, he caught his foot in a lashing and tumbled headlong into the open sea.

"Man overboard!" the cry went out.

Captain Douglas heard the call from down in his cabin. He raced to the deck as any good captain would. He took one look at his brave little boy bobbing in the powerful waves and ordered the vessel turned around. Then Captain Douglas dove overboard, without a thought for his own safety. He hit the waves and began swimming strongly, aiming himself towards his floundering son.

Meanwhile, the deckhands quickly got the lifeboat ready and put it over the side. But when the lifeboat hit the waves, it took on water and sank.

In the water, Captain Douglas was having a hard time reaching his son. No matter how hard the captain swam, the current kept taking the boy farther and farther from his grasp.

On the ship, the crew was now being kept busy holding back the captain's wife, who was determined to throw herself overboard after her husband and boy. Her screams of grief and frustration rose high over the waves like the seabird that the vessel was named after.

The *Stormy Petrel* drew closer to Captain Douglas as he swam toward his son. One crewmember threw a life belt overboard to him. The captain caught hold of the belt just as he reached his son. Captain Douglas wrapped the belt around Eddie and tried to keep the young boy's head above the water as the men hauled them back toward the ship.

The crew fought the current for over half an hour to pull the captain and the boy back on deck. By the time they got the pair on board, it was too late. Little Eddie Douglas had drowned in his father's arms. Captain Douglas tried his best to revive his son, but there was no use.

"Build two coffins," Captain Douglas ordered the ship's carpenter. "Build one small enough for my son and the other large enough to put the first coffin inside with a little room left over."

The carpenter was terrified that Douglas intended to be buried alongside his son, but nevertheless, he built the two coffins exactly as he'd been ordered to. He soon saw the wisdom behind the captain's instructions.

Then, after placing the boy's body inside the small coffin, and in turn placing that coffin inside the larger coffin, the carpenter filled the space between the two coffins with sticky pitch in order to make it airtight.

"This will keep the bad air inside the coffin during our journey," Captain Douglas explained. "I mean to see my boy is buried where he'll sleep the soundest."

When the *Stormy Petrel* sailed into Bordeaux, Captain Douglas placed his son's coffin aboard a fast-moving steamer bound for New York and made arrangements for its safe carriage home. From New York, the coffin was shipped by railcar to Nova Scotia.

Then a horse-drawn wagon carried the coffin to the Maitland cemetery, where little Eddie Douglas was finally buried.

Captain Douglas sailed the *Stormy Petrel* back to Maitland, then gave up the ship once and for all. He spent the rest of his days comforting his bereaved wife and raising their little daughter.

In the many years since Captain Douglas's own death, people have often spotted a man's figure standing over little Eddie Douglas's final resting place. Some believe that it is Captain Douglas come back from the dead to keep watch over his son. Others believe that it is the sailor who was playing with the boy right before he fell overboard. Whoever it is, the spectre still appears every once in a while to watch over the boy's grave and to remind people of the tale of the *Stormy Petrel*.

Liam and the Lutin

HAVRE BOUCHER

~

THE "LUTIN," OR "LITTLE PEOPLE," WERE A TYPE OF FAIRY-hobgoblin who reputedly came over to the New World from Old France with the first French settlers. They were believed to be both bad and good, and there wasn't much of a rule as to how they might behave. It depended upon which way the wind was blowing, I suppose. On any given day, the Lutin might helpfully shave the master's chin before he even woke from his bed, or they might shave his head instead.

The Lutin are well known in the French Shore region of Nova Scotia, where the old people still braid the manes of their horses to keep them safe from the Lutin, who are fond of tangling the horses' manes into untamable elf-locks. However, this particular tale actually comes from Havre Boucher, a small village in the belly of St. George's Bay, approximately ten kilometres west of the Canso Causeway.

Depending on who you talk to, the village of Havre Boucher is either named after its ice-locked harbour or Captain Francois Boucher of Quebec, who stayed here through the very harsh winter of 1759. Over the years, the village has served as a haven to many different groups, including a small band of surviving Acadians, a few French settlers from Arichat, and a handful of Irish families who arrived in the early 1800s.

According to legend, there was once a log chapel that sat on the western point of the harbour. The church was run by a group of French missionaries and was attended by local Mi'kmaq.

ning, the hymns were being sung, and re kept up the whole night long praying exorcising techniques on the night that the Lutin...

NAMED PLODDER

LIVED A YOUNG MAN NAMED LIAM, wn of Havre Boucher.
k," he complained to anyone who was "I live in such a very poor town in such

not have very much luck to his name. holes in his boots, and a pair of empty at, he had a rundown farm and a ram‐ ld horse named Plodder, who was his

uld go to the barn to find Plodder look‐ o matter how much he fed the old horse, he gave him, and no matter how long he looking more tired by the day. Each day lled out a little farther beneath his ratty knees bowed in more and his legs lanked ped a little lower from his big flappy lips. rse looks as if it has been out for a hard n said. "In a few more nights there will be nothing left of it but a rattling old horsehide sack wrapped around a bag of broken bones."

Then, early one morning, Liam found that Plodder's mane and tail had both been braided overnight. They were pretty braids, with long black ribbons of eel grass and ivy woven through them, but since old Plodder was built for nothing more glorified than pulling a dull plow, Liam just couldn't see the point.

That is, until he talked to his next door neighbour, Old Man Levasseur.

"Your problem is simple," Old Man Levasseur said. "Your horse is being ridden by the Lutin."

"What's a Lutin?" Liam asked.

"The Lutin are what we Acadians call faerie people," Old Man Levasseur said. "The Lutin mostly leave us people alone but they have a love of horseback riding and a fascination with the tying of knots."

"How long will this go on?" Liam asked.

"Most likely until your horse dies from exhaustion," Old Man Levasseur replied.

"Isn't there anything I can do about it?"

Old Man Levasseur shrugged and thumped his pot-belly three times fast. "Put a silver coin in a bucket and let the horse drink from it," he advised. "It is the strongest protection against the Lutin that I know of."

"And where would I find a silver coin?" Liam asked. "I barely have two brass pieces to rub together."

"Then try sprinkling some salt on the ground," Old Man Levasseur said. "The Lutin hate the salt."

"Why waste good salt on the dirt?" Liam asked.

"If you pinch your pennies any harder, the queen will blush," Old Man Levasseur teased. "Maybe you could just try setting a trap?"

Which is just what Liam did. The next evening, after putting Plodder into the stall, Liam laid seven rawhide rabbit trip-snares about the old barn in such a fashion that no matter how carefully someone approached the stall, he would be bound to catch his foot in one of the trip-snares.

However, on the next morning, Liam found that his trip-snares had been gathered up and braided into a very neat bundle. Plodder was leaning in the stall, looking even more tired than ever, with a long strand of blue jay and crow feathers woven into his braided mane and tail.

"Traps don't work," Liam told Old Man Levasseur.

"Of course they don't," Old Man Levasseur retorted. "The Lutin are far smarter than your average rabbit is."

"So what can I do?" Liam asked.

"There is another way," Old Man Levasseur said. "You're bigger than the Lutin, aren't you?"

"How would I know?" Liam said. "I've never seen a Lutin."

"Well, why don't you try catching him tonight?" Old Man Levasseur asked.

"And how do I do that?" Liam asked. "Is there a spell I should recite? Will I need to wear a crucifix or say the Lord's Prayer?"

Old Man Levasseur shrugged. "A prayer never hurt," he said. "But mostly I was just thinking you ought to sneak up and jump on his back."

Which is just what Liam set out to do.

～

MAN VERSUS LUTIN

PLODDER LOOKED GAUNTER THEN EVER BY MOONLIGHT. IT GAVE Liam a case of the bitter shivers as he stood there in the shadows of the stall. It was a good thing old Plodder was feeling so tired, because a good hard rearward kick from him might have crushed Liam's ribcage in on itself.

"This is a bad idea, isn't it, boy?" Liam whispered.

Plodder whinnied in agreement.

Going out of his way to antagonize something so magical and powerful as a Lutin certainly was a very bad idea. There was no telling what this Lutin might do to Liam if he had the notion to hurt him.

But Liam needed that horse. He was far too poor to even consider buying a new one. And besides, Plodder was the closest thing to a best friend that Liam had ever had. There was no way on this green earth that he was going to let the Lutin ride old Plodder into the dirt.

Suddenly Liam saw the tiny little Lutin creeping into the horse's stall. He looked as if he had been built from mosquito bones and cat whiskers. He was thin and wiry, with a long needle nose that looked sharp enough to serve as a stinger. He had a nasty little sneer that looked to have been carved onto his tiny leather face. His skin was dusty grey, tinged with a hint of river moss. The only spot of colour upon the Lutin's entire body was a bright red cap that perched nattily upon his head.

Liam waited patiently. He knew that he would only get one chance at catching this little man.

The Lutin tiptoed closer and then all at once he leaped upon Plodder and kicked him in the ribs with a pair of heels that looked as sharp as hunting knives.

Liam leapt too. He grabbed hold of the Lutin, but touching him was as painful as picking up a mid-summer hornet nest. Liam screamed and tried to pull his hands free, but the Lutin braided Liam's fingers into Plodder's mane in less time than it might take you to take a good deep breath.

"Help!" Liam yelled.

Suddenly, Old Plodder reared up and leaped clear over the stall gate, dusting the cobwebs from the barn rafters. The barn doors flew open before the horse, as if they'd been kicked.

Liam squeezed the Lutin harder. No matter how much hanging on hurt, he was determined not to let go.

"Set me free!" the Lutin shrieked.

"Leave go of my horse," Liam said. "Or I'll squeeze you until your eyes bleed."

"Then ride with me," the Lutin said in a voice that sounded like a pit saw crossed with squeaky chalk. "And I will show you a treasure beyond your wildest of dreams."

And Plodder took off galloping.

～

LIAM'S LONG MIDNIGHT RIDE

LIAM HAD NEVER SEEN A HORSE GALLOP SO HARD AND SO FAST. Plodder hit the Strait of Canso and leaped over it. Liam took a panic stricken half-second blink at the water surging below him and braced for the impact of the inevitable landing to come. Only the landing never happened.

Old Plodder must have been crossed with mythical Pegasus himself, because instead of falling, the old nag rose higher and higher into the night sky, nearly flying headlong into a great horned owl.

"Whoo-hoo-hoo-hoo," said the great horned owl. "Whooo, whooo?"

"Me!" shouted Liam.

"Take a look down, why don't you?" the Lutin asked. "And forget about your bird watching."

Liam looked down in time to see a great beast rearing up out of a patch of ground so pitchy black that it seemed to suck the starlight out of the night sky. Three old hags danced at his feet.

"That's the Bochdan of the Black Ground," the Lutin said. "And his three sisters."

And from underneath the shadow of the Bochdan purred a big fat old black pussy cat. "Hey, Mister Coal Shadow!" the Lutin called out.

The Lutin rode old Plodder even harder. The ground whizzed by below them.

"Slow down!" Liam called out.

"We're only getting started," the Lutin replied.

Farther up the coastline, Liam stared down at what looked to be a legion of devils marching down into a coal mine with picks upon their shoulders. Mermaids and selkies waved at him from the waves as he flew by. A sea monster roared up out of the water and playfully splashed him.

"Look over here," the Lutin sang out and pointed.

Liam looked in wonder as the Capstick Bigfoot stepped out of the woods and blinked up at them with his big beautiful soft brown eyes. Farther along, a shape that was small, sad, and lonely waved a flipper their way from the storm-tossed waters off Port Hood.

"How's that for a grand tour?" the Lutin shouted as they soared along over a stretch of the Northumberland Strait. The entire crew of the Phantom Ship toasted Liam, the Lutin, and Plodder as they passed overhead, raising great flaming flagons of hot spiced rum to the night sky.

Five babies waved their tiny thin-boned fingers from out of the dirt of the New Glasgow cemetery. The *Favourite* rose and sank again in the belly of Pictou Harbour. A bridge screeched at Liam and the Lutin as they flew past Parrsboro. The Kentville artist stood up and waved his paintbrush. Flames from Amherst and Caledonia Mills lit the midnight heavens. Curtains blew and ships sank and buried treasure twinkled from below and Ivy threw a spoon. The werewolf howled and Sophie's ghost wailed and the spirit of Captain Kidd laughed out loud and danced a jig with the Lady in Blue.

"Here we go now," the Lutin shrieked as they passed over McNabs Island and raced neck and neck with a galloping ghostly mare.

Then he turned the horse in a hard left and headed back up toward Cape Breton, where he pulled old Plodder down to the earth, just outside of Liam's ramshackle barn.

"Home again, home again, jiggedy-jig," said the Lutin.

"And where is my treasure?" Liam asked.

"Were you not looking as we flew?" the Lutin asked. "Were you that terrified that you closed your eyes tight?"

"I kept them open," Liam said. "And all I saw was a bunch of old ghost stories."

"That's the life and breath of this land you live in," the Lutin replied. "No greater treasure can be found beyond a country's folklore."

"Well that's all well and good," said Liam disgustedly. "But I'm still out a very good horse."

The Lutin looked at Plodder, who was still gasping and wheezing and very nearly at death's dark doorway.

"I don't think he was all that much to begin with," the Lutin pointed out.

"Maybe not," Liam said. "But Plodder has carried me for many a year. He has pulled my plow and filled my larder. I have laughed with that old horse and I have cried with him and there are more stories than I could ever remember that begin and end with that horse, who happens to be my very best friend."

The Lutin thought about that. "Fair enough," he finally said. And then he stood up on tiptoe, somehow stretching his tiny body high enough to reach old Plodder's left nostril. He blew a strong breath into the nostril and Plodder swelled up like an inflated bladder-float.

"Stop that!" Liam said in panic.

But the Lutin blew two more times. At the third blow in, Plodder snorted back out. He shook his body like a wet dog and every wrinkle and crease on that poor old nag flew off like it was nothing more than a handful of lint.

When the horse quit his shaking, Liam couldn't believe his eyes. There, standing before him, was Plodder, only years and years younger, looking stronger and faster than he had been in a long, long time.

"There," the Lutin said. And then he loaded two large sacks upon Plodder's back.

"That's all the gold that you will ever need to live off," the Lutin said. "Now what I want you to do is to ride out across the province and tell all the stories that I showed you tonight on that long gallop of ours. I want you to tell each story the best way you can, and if you can't remember a detail, feel free to make it up."

And that's just what Liam did.

OTHER BOOKS BY
Steve Vernon

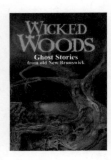

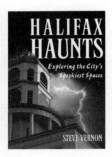